4 5 billion years ago, our planet, Earth, forms.

3 1 billion years after the Big Bang, the galaxies begin to take shape.

8 2.5 billion years ago, our breathable atmosphere forms.

7 3 billion years ago, life begins with the appearance of the first bacteria and blue algae.

Tyrannosaurus

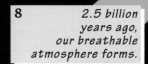
Argentinosaurus

Baryonyx

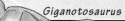
Triceratops

Vol. 6

Camarasaurus

Vol. 5

Vol. 4

Cretaceous

Scipionyx

Giganotosaurus

CONTENTS

First published in the United States of America in 2008 by Abbeville Press, 137 Varick Street, New York, NY 10013

First published in Italy in 2008 by Editoriale Jaca Book S.p.A., via Frua 11, 20146 Milano

First edition
10 9 8 7 6 5 4 3 2 1

Library of Congress Cataloging-in-Publication Data
Bacchin, Matteo.
  [Marcia. English]
  The journey : Plateosaurus / drawings and story Matteo Bacchin ; essays and story Marco Signore ; translated from the Italian by Marguerite Shore.
    p. cm. — (Dinosaurs)
  Originally published: La Marcia : Triassico : nuove orme su Pangea. Milano : Editoriale Jaca Book, 2008.
  ISBN 978-0-7892-0978-8 (hardcover : alk. paper) 1. Plateosaurus—Juvenile literature. 2. Dinosaurs—Juvenile literature. 3. Paleontology—Triassic—Juvenile literature. 4. Paleogeography—Triassic—Juvenile literature. I. Signore, Marco. II. Title. III. Title: Plateosaurus.

  QE862.S3B33 2008
  560'.1762—dc22

                    2008007611

For bulk and premium sales and for text adoption procedures, write to Customer Service Manager, Abbeville Press, 137 Varick Street, New York, NY 10013, or call 1-800-ARTBOOK.

Visit Abbeville Press online at www.abbeville.com.

For the English-language edition: David Fabricant, editor; Ashley Benning, copy editor; Austin Allen, production editor; Louise Kurtz, production manager; Robert Weisberg, composition; Misha Beletsky, cover design and typography.

Foreword
By Mark Norell

Anyone reading a book like this has probably watched his or her share of nature programs. In HDTV, we see thousands of East African ungulates migrating across the plains of Tsavo, tigers exterminating goats in India, and life beneath the Antarctic ice as captured on critter cam. But it is difficult to visualize how the landscapes inhabited by prehistoric animals appeared. A comparable example is the recent past. It is safe to say that when most of us conjure up Europe in the Dark Ages, it is a lightless, gloomy place, even though much of it was located on the sunny shores of the Mediterranean! Which brings me back to dinosaurs and *The Journey*.

There are as many ways to think about dinosaurs and how they lived as there are types of dinosaurs that have been discovered. This group of animals has navigated our planet's topography for 235 million years. (Yes, they still exist—we just call them birds now.) Modern birds, and many of the extinct traditional dinosaurs, have explored almost every ecological niche available. Their diversity of body plans eclipses even that of modern mammals (at least in the terrestrial realm). The bee hummingbird, which is able to perch on a pencil eraser, is one of the smallest warm-blooded animals, weighing only one-sixteenth of an ounce. The gigantic *Argentinosaurus* (which lived 100 million years ago in Patagonia) may have reached over 40 yards in length and weighed more than 10 African elephants.

Our knowledge of the dinosaurs of the past has increased geometrically in the past two decades. We now know for certain that these animals lived at latitudes above the polar circles. They raced through dense subtropical rain forests and achieved impressive population densities in primordial savannahs. It would not have been unusual to see herds of giant dinosaurs walking on sandy beaches or nesting in upland dune fields.

Here in *The Journey*, you will see a dramatized yet accurate portrayal of dinosaur life—a life that is often difficult to imagine from the fossils, however painstakingly excavated and exhibited. But think of them as they were, imagined through the lens of the present—living, breathing, mating creatures enjoying blue skies, torrential rain, intense heat, nice beaches, and broad vistas. If you want to know what the dinosaurs' world was like, just look around. Next time you see a nature show on television, just exchange the present-day animals for dinosaurs, and you will see a story very much like the one you are about to encounter.

DINOSAURS

The Journey
PLATEOSAURUS

Drawings and story
MATTEO BACCHIN

Essays and story
MARCO SIGNORE

Translated from the Italian by Marguerite Shore

ABBEVILLE KIDS
A Division of Abbeville Publishing Group

New York London

IN THIS STORY

1 *Plateosaurus*

2 *Liliensternus*

3 *Eudimorphodon*

4 *Shastasauridae*

5 *Hyperodapedon*

6 *Nothosaurus*

7 *Oligokyphus*

8 *Peteinosaurus*

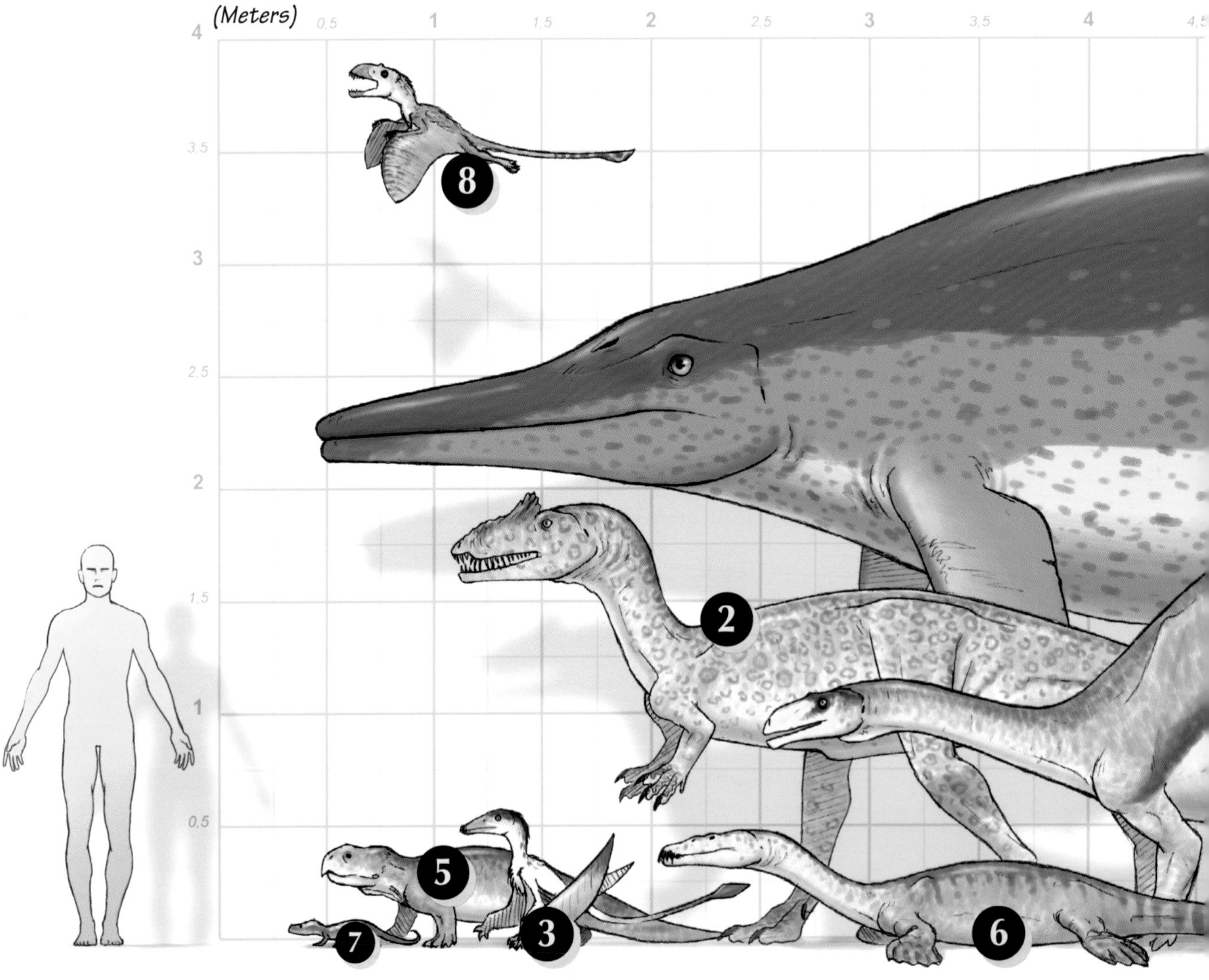

(Meters)

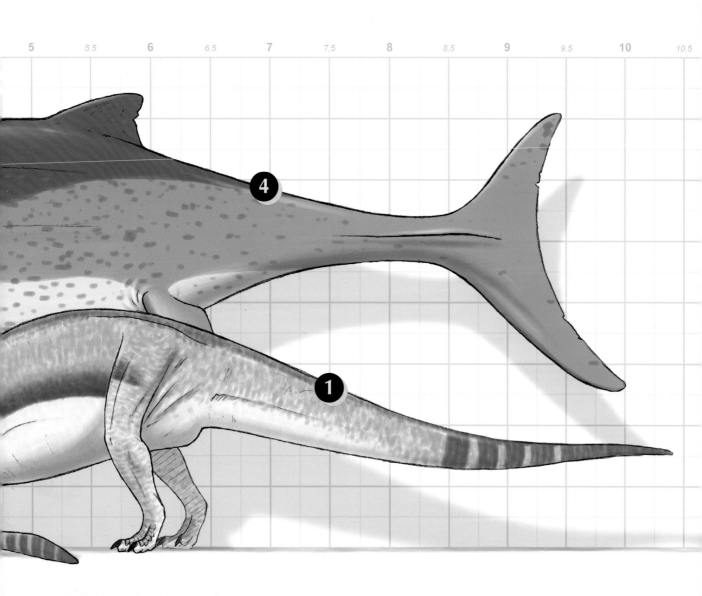

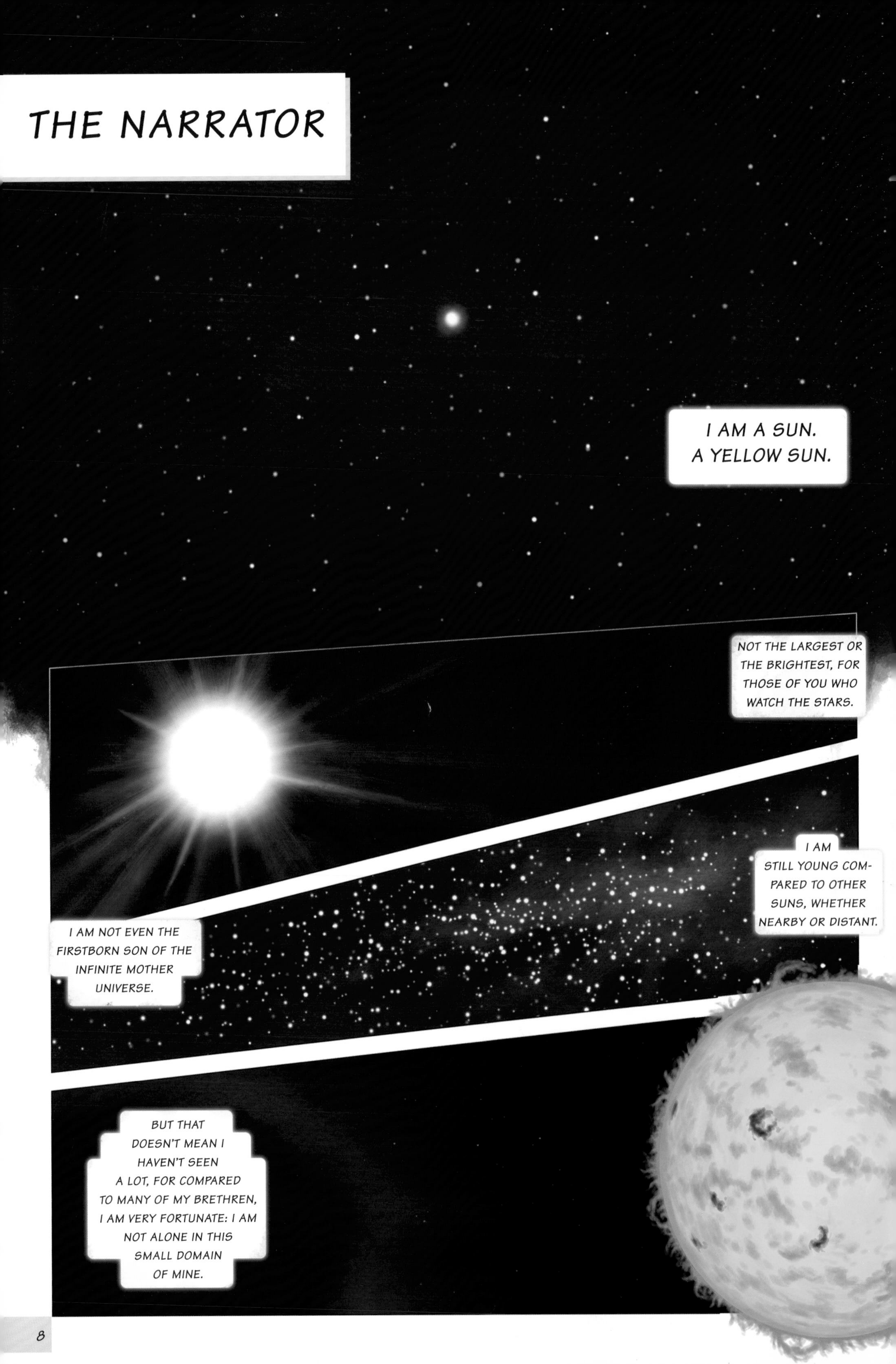

THE NARRATOR

I AM A SUN.
A YELLOW SUN.

NOT THE LARGEST OR
THE BRIGHTEST, FOR
THOSE OF YOU WHO
WATCH THE STARS.

I AM
STILL YOUNG COM-
PARED TO OTHER
SUNS, WHETHER
NEARBY OR DISTANT.

I AM NOT EVEN THE
FIRSTBORN SON OF THE
INFINITE MOTHER
UNIVERSE.

BUT THAT
DOESN'T MEAN I
HAVEN'T SEEN
A LOT, FOR COMPARED
TO MANY OF MY BRETHREN,
I AM VERY FORTUNATE: I AM
NOT ALONE IN THIS
SMALL DOMAIN
OF MINE.

DIFFERENT WORLDS HAVE FORMED AROUND ME, AND I HAVE WITNESSED MANY DIFFERENT LIVES IN THE TIME I HAVE BEEN GRANTED THUS FAR.

AND I WANT TO TELL YOU A STORY PRECISELY ABOUT ONE OF THESE EXCEPTIONAL LIVES. MY STORY TAKES PLACE IN PERHAPS THE MOST SPECTACULAR AND THRIVING PERIOD THAT THE EARTH, THE THIRD STAR AND JEWEL AMONG ALL OTHERS, HAS EVER EXPERIENCED, TAKING ADVANTAGE OF MY LIGHT.

IN ROCK AMONG THE ROCKS,

MOMENTS CAPTURED IN STONE—TRACES OF THAT PAST ERA AND THE BEINGS THAT LIVED THEN.

A PERIOD OF WHICH YOU HUMANS HAVE REDISCOVERED LOST MEMORIES

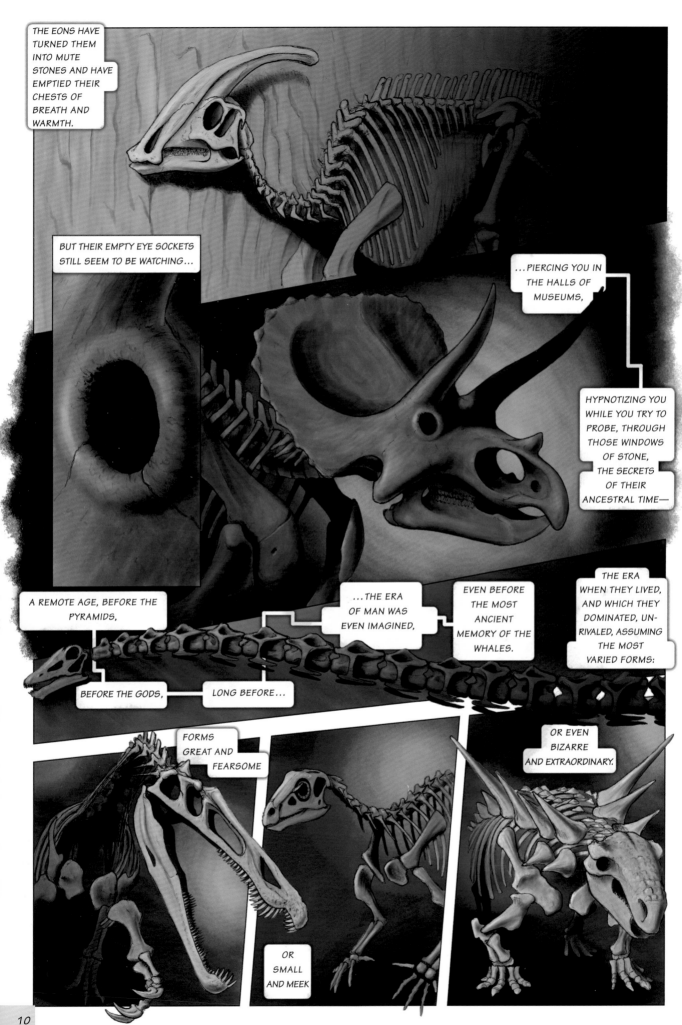

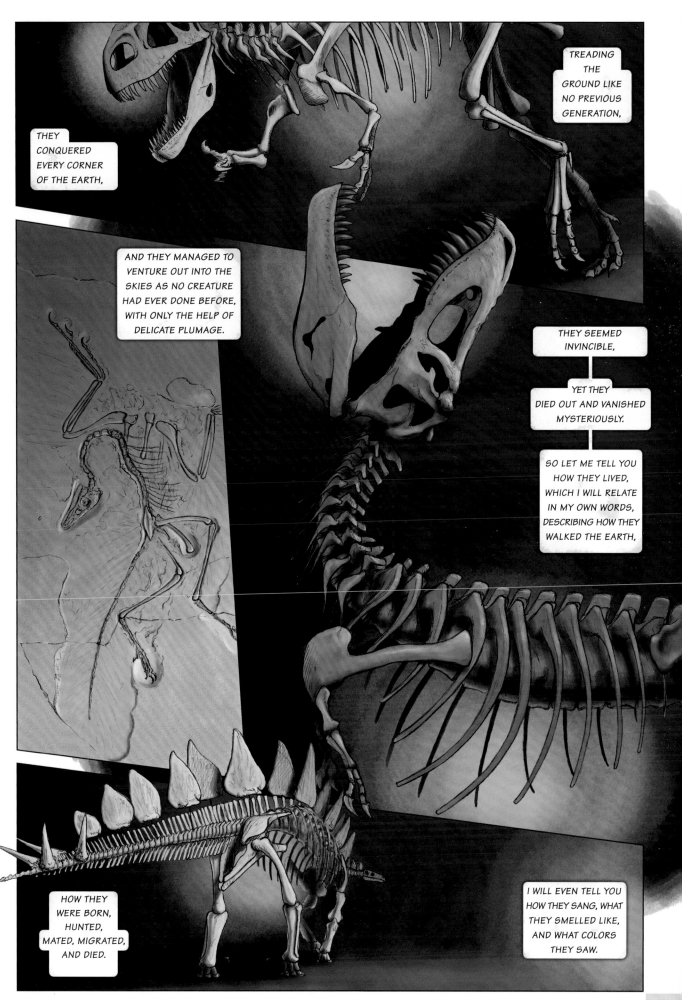

1 THE JOURNEY

ON EARTH, ALL THINGS COME FROM THE SEA,

JUST AS THE FIRST STORY I WANT TO TELL YOU BEGINS IN THE SEA.

IT UNFOLDS DURING AN ERA OF NEW TRACKS, WHEN THE DINOSAURS BEGAN TO SPREAD OVER THE EARTH, LEAVING BIRDLIKE PRINTS, THE LIKES OF WHICH HAD NEVER BEEN SEEN BEFORE.

MORE PRECISELY, THIS STORY BEGINS WHERE THE DARK ROCKS OF A CONTINENT ENCOUNTER A TROPICAL OCEAN...

... THAT HAD OPENED UP MILLIONS OF YEARS BEFORE THE NEW TRACKS APPEARED, SEPARATING A SINGLE, BOUNDLESS EXPANSE OF LAND INTO TWO HALVES.

I THINK YOU WILL BE SURPRISED TO LEARN THAT THIS GREAT SEA, WARM AND CRYSTAL CLEAR, WAS NOT LOCATED IN THE BALMY SOUTHERN LATITUDES.

THE FOAMY WAVES OF THIS OCEAN BROKE ALONG THE COASTS OF A LAND THAT IN YOUR TIME, YOU WILL CALL SWITZERLAND.

IN FACT, I THINK THAT IF YOU HAD SEEN THE EARTH AT THAT TIME, FROM MY VANTAGE POINT, YOU WOULD BARELY HAVE RECOGNIZED IT.

THERE, WHERE TODAY YOU WOULD FIND GREEN PASTURES AND TALL, SNOW-COVERED MOUNTAINS, IN THE ERA OF THE NEW TRACKS AN ANCIENT OCEAN TEEMED WITH SILVERY FISH.

NEAR THESE SHORES, YOU WOULD DOUBT-LESS HAVE SPOTTED SOME OF THE ENORMOUS INHABITANTS OF THE SEA AS THEY CAME TO THE SURFACE, PANTING FOR BREATH.

LIKE THE DOLPHINS OF YOUR ERA, WHICH THEY RESEMBLE, THESE LIZARD-FISH HAD TO BREATHE THE SAME AIR YOU DO IN ORDER TO SURVIVE.

OVER THE AGES, THEIR SUPPLE BODIES HAD BECOME PERFECT FOR SWIMMING, THEIR PAWS CHANGING INTO FINS.

THEY GATHERED IN GROUPS IN THESE FISH-FILLED WATERS FOR SUMPTUOUS BANQUETS.

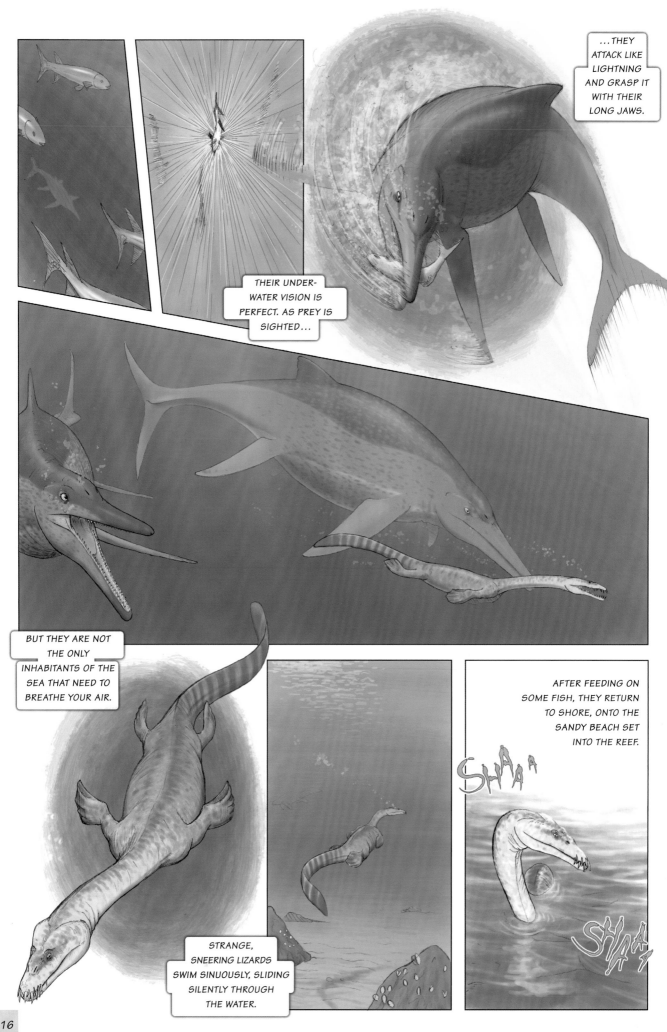

...THEY ATTACK LIKE LIGHTNING AND GRASP IT WITH THEIR LONG JAWS.

THEIR UNDER-WATER VISION IS PERFECT. AS PREY IS SIGHTED...

BUT THEY ARE NOT THE ONLY INHABITANTS OF THE SEA THAT NEED TO BREATHE YOUR AIR.

AFTER FEEDING ON SOME FISH, THEY RETURN TO SHORE, ONTO THE SANDY BEACH SET INTO THE REEF.

STRANGE, SNEERING LIZARDS SWIM SINUOUSLY, SLIDING SILENTLY THROUGH THE WATER.

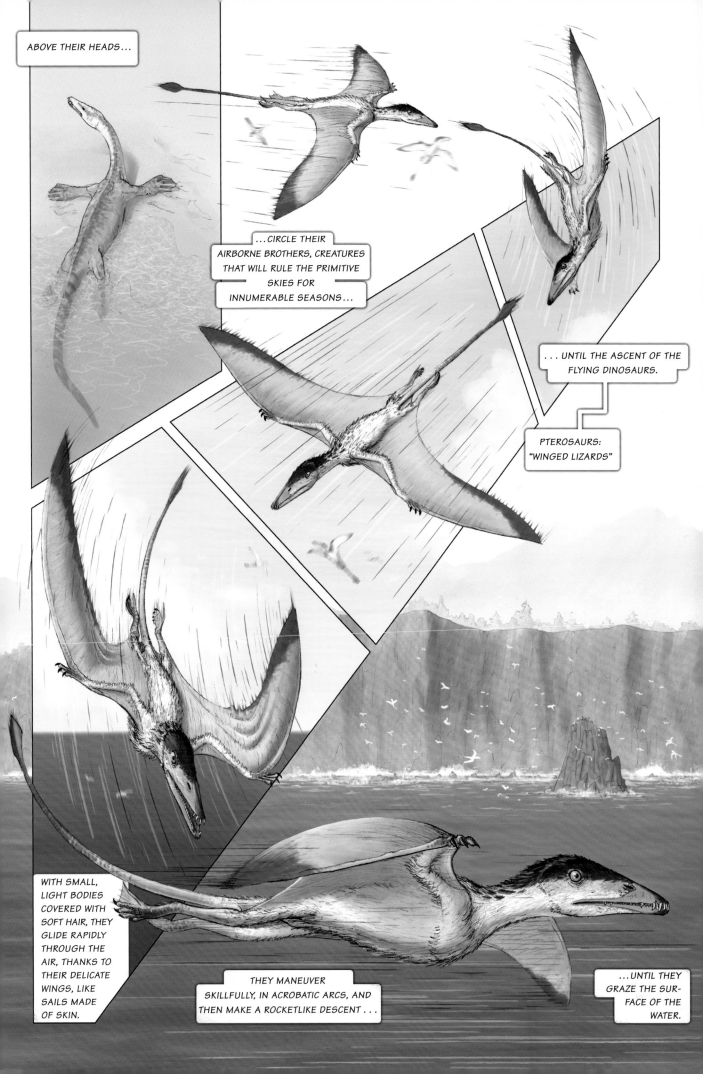

THEIR LARGE, ROUND, SHINY EYES FOCUS...

...IN ORDER TO SPOT THE SMALLEST SILVERY GLIMMER IN THE DARK BLUE WATER.

THEIR NEEDLE-POINTED TEETH WAIT TO SNATCH A VICTIM...

CATCH!

...AND WITH A JERK OF HIS TRIANGULAR HEAD, ONE LITTLE BROTHER OF THE WIND CLASPS A SHINY LITTLE FISH IN HIS BEAK.

!

FLAP

FLAP

FLAP

A BEAT OF HIS WINGS CARRIES HIM ALOFT AGAIN— POETRY IN MOTION.

THESE SMALL ANIMALS NEST AMID THE ROCKS OF THE REEF, OR IN THE TREES THAT DOT THE SHORE.

18

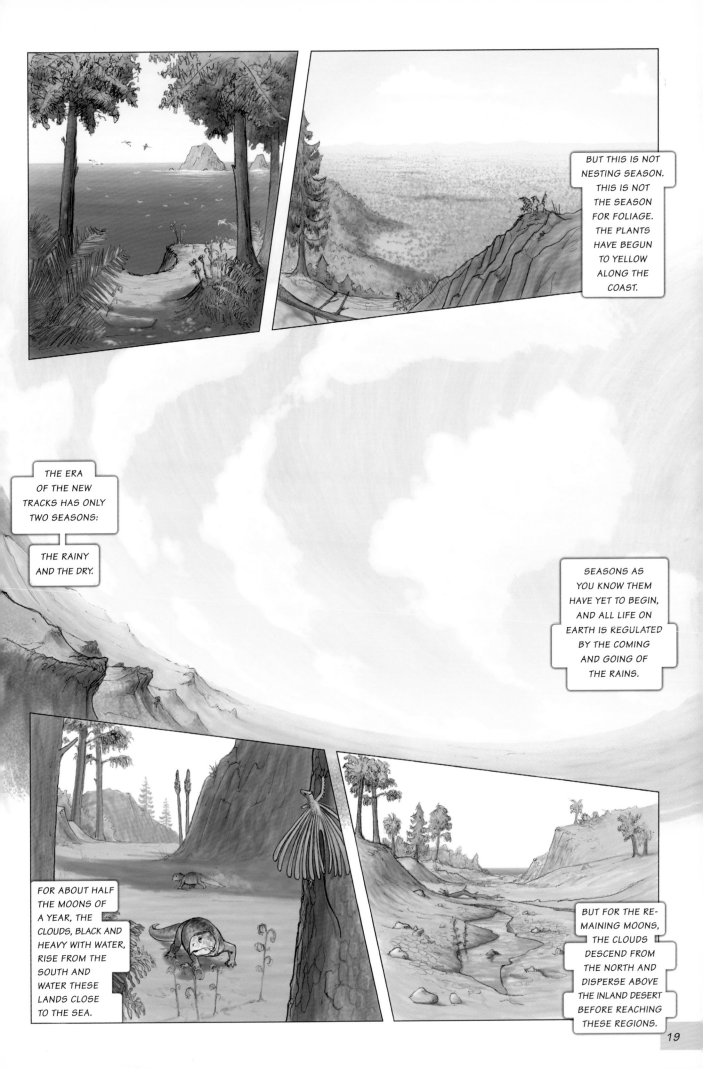

BUT THIS IS NOT NESTING SEASON. THIS IS NOT THE SEASON FOR FOLIAGE. THE PLANTS HAVE BEGUN TO YELLOW ALONG THE COAST.

THE ERA OF THE NEW TRACKS HAS ONLY TWO SEASONS:

THE RAINY AND THE DRY.

SEASONS AS YOU KNOW THEM HAVE YET TO BEGIN, AND ALL LIFE ON EARTH IS REGULATED BY THE COMING AND GOING OF THE RAINS.

FOR ABOUT HALF THE MOONS OF A YEAR, THE CLOUDS, BLACK AND HEAVY WITH WATER, RISE FROM THE SOUTH AND WATER THESE LANDS CLOSE TO THE SEA.

BUT FOR THE RE-MAINING MOONS, THE CLOUDS DESCEND FROM THE NORTH AND DISPERSE ABOVE THE INLAND DESERT BEFORE REACHING THESE REGIONS.

19

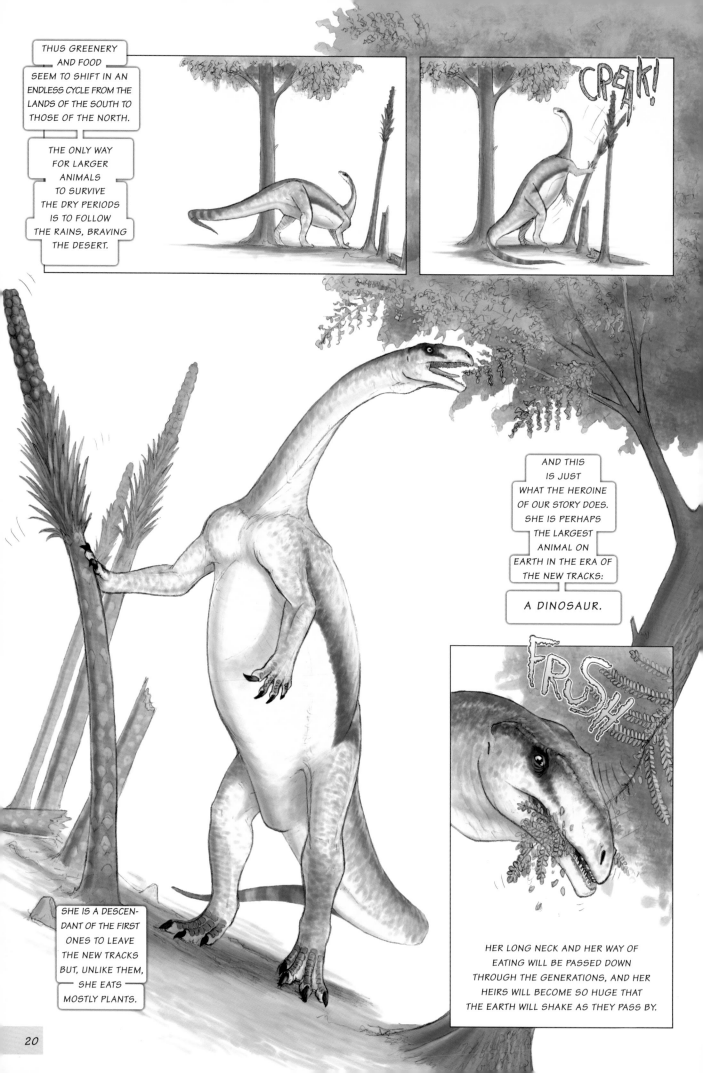

THUS GREENERY AND FOOD SEEM TO SHIFT IN AN ENDLESS CYCLE FROM THE LANDS OF THE SOUTH TO THOSE OF THE NORTH.

THE ONLY WAY FOR LARGER ANIMALS TO SURVIVE THE DRY PERIODS IS TO FOLLOW THE RAINS, BRAVING THE DESERT.

CREAK!

AND THIS IS JUST WHAT THE HEROINE OF OUR STORY DOES. SHE IS PERHAPS THE LARGEST ANIMAL ON EARTH IN THE ERA OF THE NEW TRACKS:

A DINOSAUR.

FRUSH

SHE IS A DESCENDANT OF THE FIRST ONES TO LEAVE THE NEW TRACKS BUT, UNLIKE THEM, SHE EATS MOSTLY PLANTS.

HER LONG NECK AND HER WAY OF EATING WILL BE PASSED DOWN THROUGH THE GENERATIONS, AND HER HEIRS WILL BECOME SO HUGE THAT THE EARTH WILL SHAKE AS THEY PASS BY.

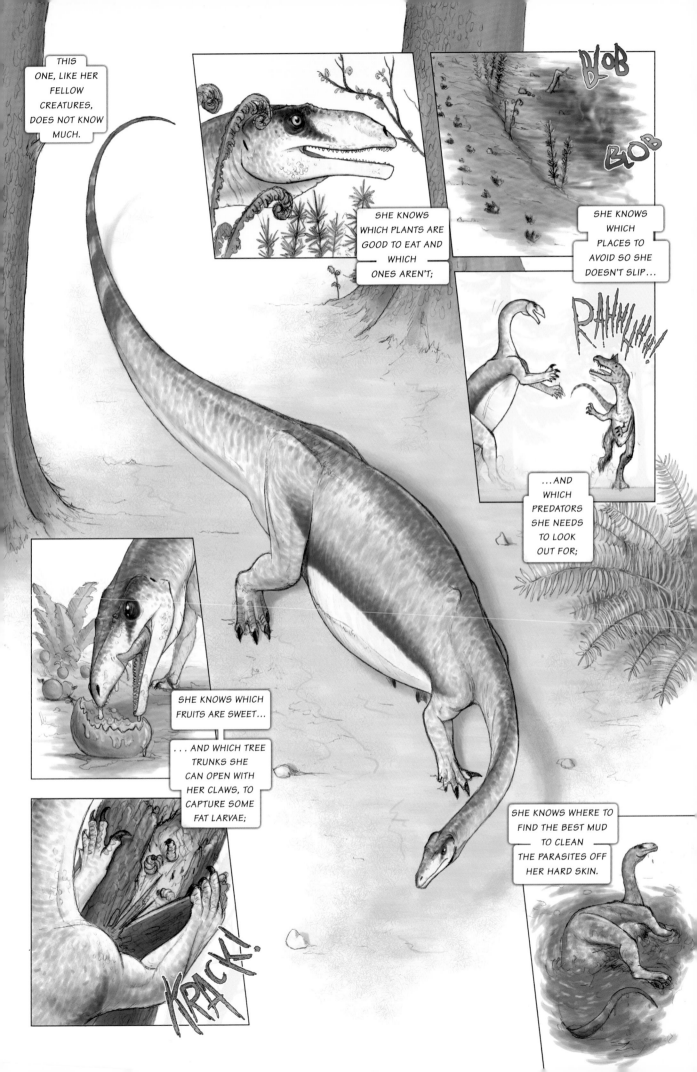

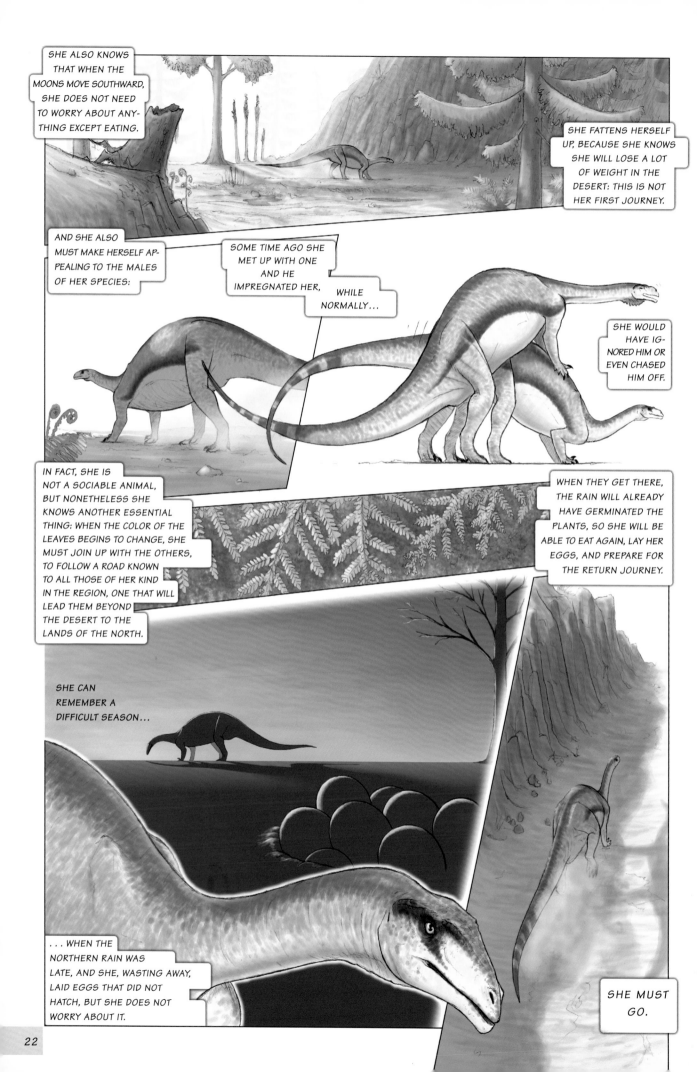

SHE ALSO KNOWS THAT WHEN THE MOONS MOVE SOUTHWARD, SHE DOES NOT NEED TO WORRY ABOUT ANYTHING EXCEPT EATING.

SHE FATTENS HERSELF UP, BECAUSE SHE KNOWS SHE WILL LOSE A LOT OF WEIGHT IN THE DESERT: THIS IS NOT HER FIRST JOURNEY.

AND SHE ALSO MUST MAKE HERSELF APPEALING TO THE MALES OF HER SPECIES:

SOME TIME AGO SHE MET UP WITH ONE AND HE IMPREGNATED HER, WHILE NORMALLY...

SHE WOULD HAVE IGNORED HIM OR EVEN CHASED HIM OFF.

IN FACT, SHE IS NOT A SOCIABLE ANIMAL, BUT NONETHELESS SHE KNOWS ANOTHER ESSENTIAL THING: WHEN THE COLOR OF THE LEAVES BEGINS TO CHANGE, SHE MUST JOIN UP WITH THE OTHERS, TO FOLLOW A ROAD KNOWN TO ALL THOSE OF HER KIND IN THE REGION, ONE THAT WILL LEAD THEM BEYOND THE DESERT TO THE LANDS OF THE NORTH.

WHEN THEY GET THERE, THE RAIN WILL ALREADY HAVE GERMINATED THE PLANTS, SO SHE WILL BE ABLE TO EAT AGAIN, LAY HER EGGS, AND PREPARE FOR THE RETURN JOURNEY.

SHE CAN REMEMBER A DIFFICULT SEASON...

...WHEN THE NORTHERN RAIN WAS LATE, AND SHE, WASTING AWAY, LAID EGGS THAT DID NOT HATCH, BUT SHE DOES NOT WORRY ABOUT IT.

SHE MUST GO.

THE FIRST PART OF THE JOURNEY RUNS THROUGH THE FOREST.

THE PLANTS ARE A BIT DRY, BUT IF SHE SEES ANY FERNS THAT ARE GOOD ENOUGH, SHE WILL NOT PASS THEM BY.

SHE SEES ONE, AND SHE ALSO SEES A YOUNG MALE BITING INTO IT.

GROOOOOOOAGH

SHE CHARGES, CHASING HIM OFF.

GRRRR

URK URK

SNAP

SHE DEVOURS THE YELLOWED FERN AS IF SHE HADN'T EATEN FOR DAYS,

AND STARTS AGAIN...

...SHE MUST KEEP MOVING.

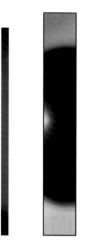

WHEN THE JOURNEY REACHES THE GREAT DESERT, SEVERAL DAYS HAVE ALREADY GONE BY.

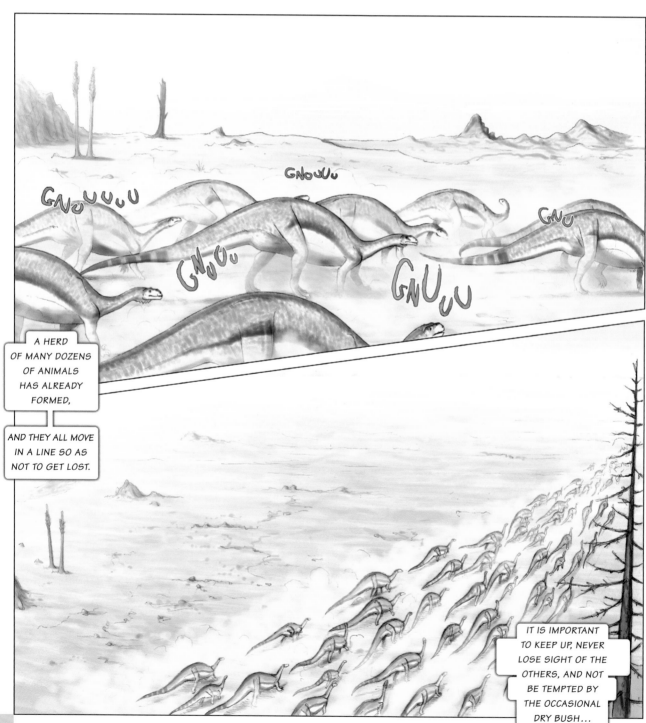

GNOUUUU

GNOUUU

GNUUU

GNUU

GNUUU

GNU

A HERD OF MANY DOZENS OF ANIMALS HAS ALREADY FORMED,

AND THEY ALL MOVE IN A LINE SO AS NOT TO GET LOST.

IT IS IMPORTANT TO KEEP UP, NEVER LOSE SIGHT OF THE OTHERS, AND NOT BE TEMPTED BY THE OCCASIONAL DRY BUSH...

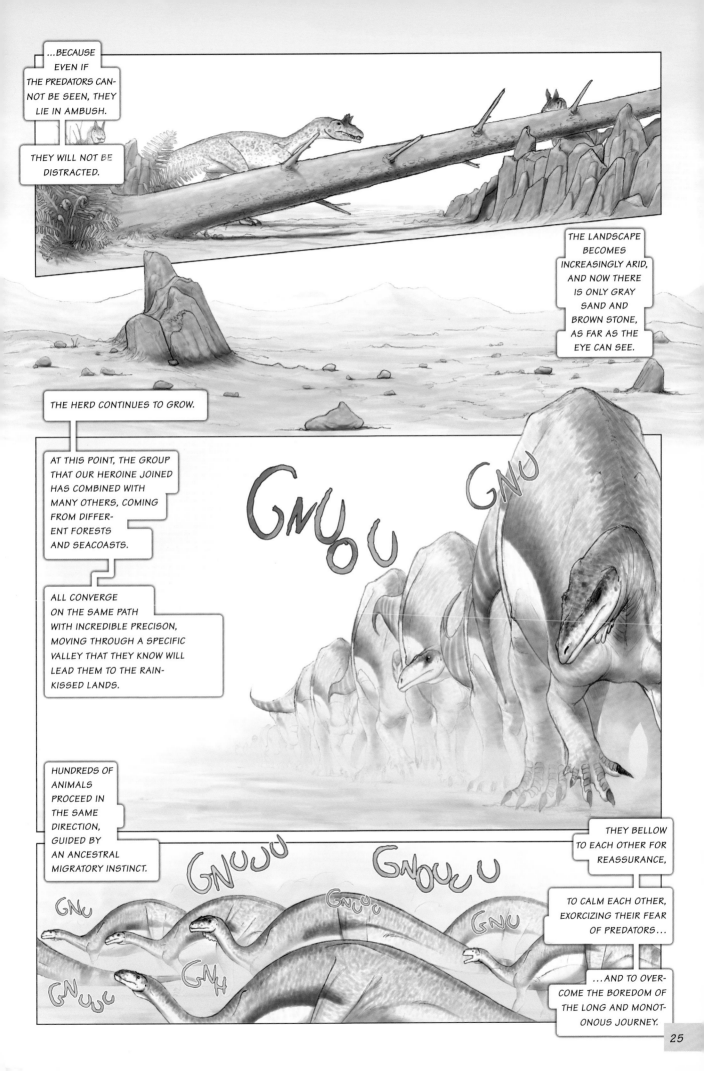

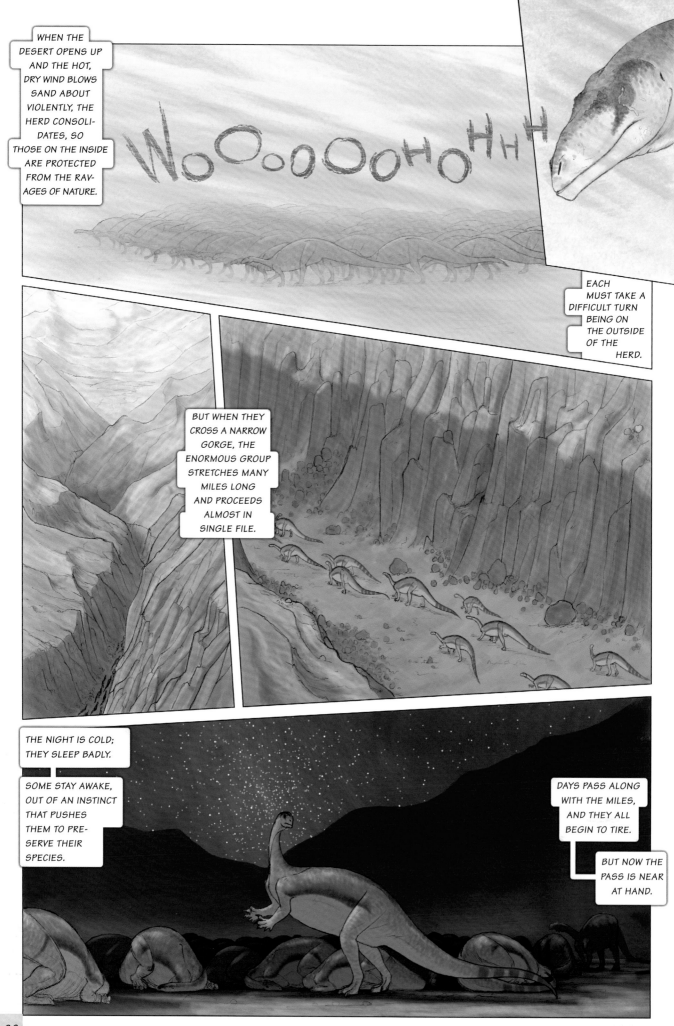

WHEN THE DESERT OPENS UP AND THE HOT, DRY WIND BLOWS SAND ABOUT VIOLENTLY, THE HERD CONSOLIDATES, SO THOSE ON THE INSIDE ARE PROTECTED FROM THE RAVAGES OF NATURE.

WOOOOOOHHH

EACH MUST TAKE A DIFFICULT TURN BEING ON THE OUTSIDE OF THE HERD.

BUT WHEN THEY CROSS A NARROW GORGE, THE ENORMOUS GROUP STRETCHES MANY MILES LONG AND PROCEEDS ALMOST IN SINGLE FILE.

THE NIGHT IS COLD; THEY SLEEP BADLY.

SOME STAY AWAKE, OUT OF AN INSTINCT THAT PUSHES THEM TO PRESERVE THEIR SPECIES.

DAYS PASS ALONG WITH THE MILES, AND THEY ALL BEGIN TO TIRE.

BUT NOW THE PASS IS NEAR AT HAND.

THE LONG JOURNEY RESUMES, ALWAYS AT THE FIRST LIGHT OF DAWN.

IN THE COLD, THIN MOUNTAIN AIR, THE HUGE ANIMALS SCRAMBLE ALONG A NARROW, ROCKY PATH,

A PATH THAT GENERATIONS OF THEIR ANCESTORS HAVE TRACED, COMING AND GOING FROM SOUTH TO NORTH.

SOME, THE LEAST EX-
PERIENCED OR MOST
EMACIATED BY THE
LONG TREK, STUMBLE AND
SLIDE DOWN BELOW.

IF THEIR
NECKS
BREAK, THEY
ARE LUCKY.

MANY,
INSTEAD,
ARE UNLUCKY
ENOUGH TO
BREAK ONLY
A PAW...

...SO THEY
SEE THE
CARNIVORES
APPROACHING
THEM.

THEIR
COMPANIONS
WALK ON,
KNOWING THAT
THE SACRIFICE
OF A FEW WILL
ALLOW MANY TO
CONTINUE.

AT FIRST THE PASS BECOMES INCREASINGLY NARROW AND SHADOWED,

BUT IT WIDENS AGAIN, AND THE HERD SENSES THE JOURNEY GETTING EASIER.

YES, THEY ARE DESCENDING.

IN FACT, THEY CAN ALREADY SMELL THE SCENT OF SUCCULENT GREENERY,

PREVIOUSLY BLOCKED OUT BY THE ROCKY AND IMPOSING HIGHLANDS.

NOW THEY NEED TO TRAVEL ONLY ONE MORE MILE BEFORE THEY CAN SEE THE DESERT BLOOMING IN INCREASING ABUNDANCE.

29

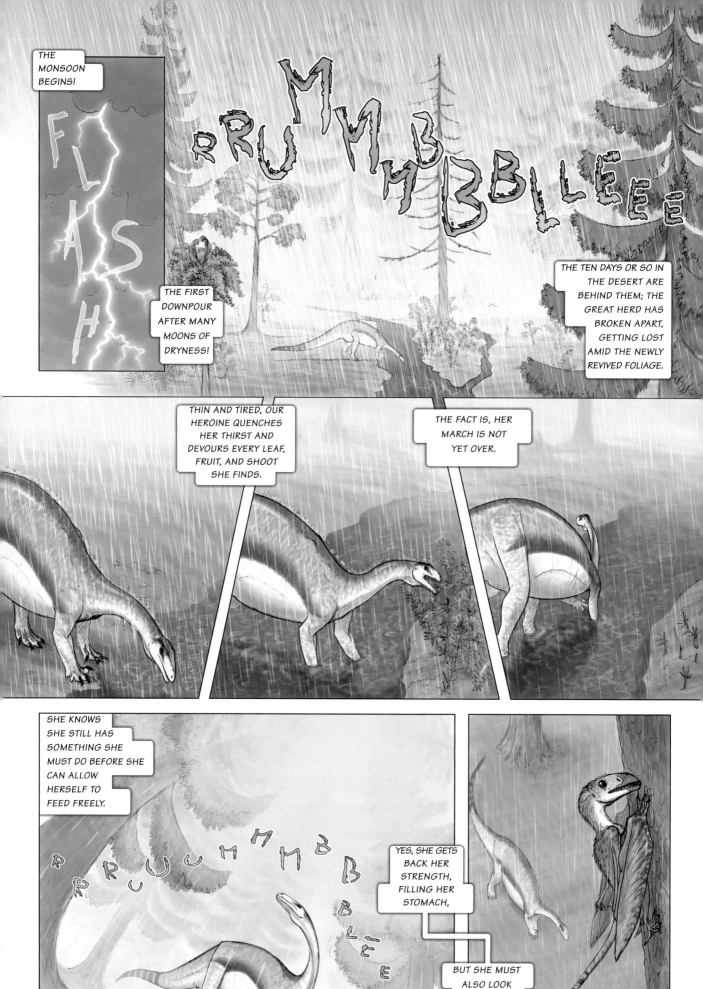

THE MONSOON BEGINS!

FLASH

RRUMMBMMBBLLEEE

THE FIRST DOWNPOUR AFTER MANY MOONS OF DRYNESS!

THE TEN DAYS OR SO IN THE DESERT ARE BEHIND THEM; THE GREAT HERD HAS BROKEN APART, GETTING LOST AMID THE NEWLY REVIVED FOLIAGE.

THIN AND TIRED, OUR HEROINE QUENCHES HER THIRST AND DEVOURS EVERY LEAF, FRUIT, AND SHOOT SHE FINDS.

THE FACT IS, HER MARCH IS NOT YET OVER.

SHE KNOWS SHE STILL HAS SOMETHING SHE MUST DO BEFORE SHE CAN ALLOW HERSELF TO FEED FREELY.

RRUUMMBBLLEEE

YES, SHE GETS BACK HER STRENGTH, FILLING HER STOMACH,

BUT SHE MUST ALSO LOOK FOR THE RIGHT PLACE TO LAY HER EGGS.

30

SHE FINDS IT BENEATH AN ENORMOUS, ANCIENT CONIFER.

SHE DIGS HER NEST WITH HER PAWS.

IT NEEDS TO BE JUST THE RIGHT DEPTH, OR THE LITTLE ONES WON'T BE ABLE TO GET OUT.

SHE HAS ALREADY DONE THIS, OTHER TIMES, BUT IT WAS DIFFICULT TO LEARN.

RASP!

RASP!

WHEN THE HOLE IS READY, SHE LOWERS HER BELLY AND DEPOSITS A DOZEN SPECKLED SPHERES, AS DELI-CATE AS PORCELAIN.

THESE ARE HER EGGS, WHICH HAVE BEEN GROWING INSIDE HER OVER THE RECENT MOONS.

HAVING LAID THEM ALL, SHE CAREFULLY SHIFTS SOME WITH HER SNOUT, ARRANGING THEM INSTINCTIVELY.

THEN SHE COVERS THEM WITH DARK EARTH, LEAVES, AND BRANCHES TO KEEP THEM WARM.

SHE WILL WAIT FOR THE EGGS TO HATCH, STAYING FOR SOME TIME IN THE SURROUNDING AREA, KEEPING WATCH OVER THE NEST SO IT IS NOT PLUNDERED.

BARG!!!

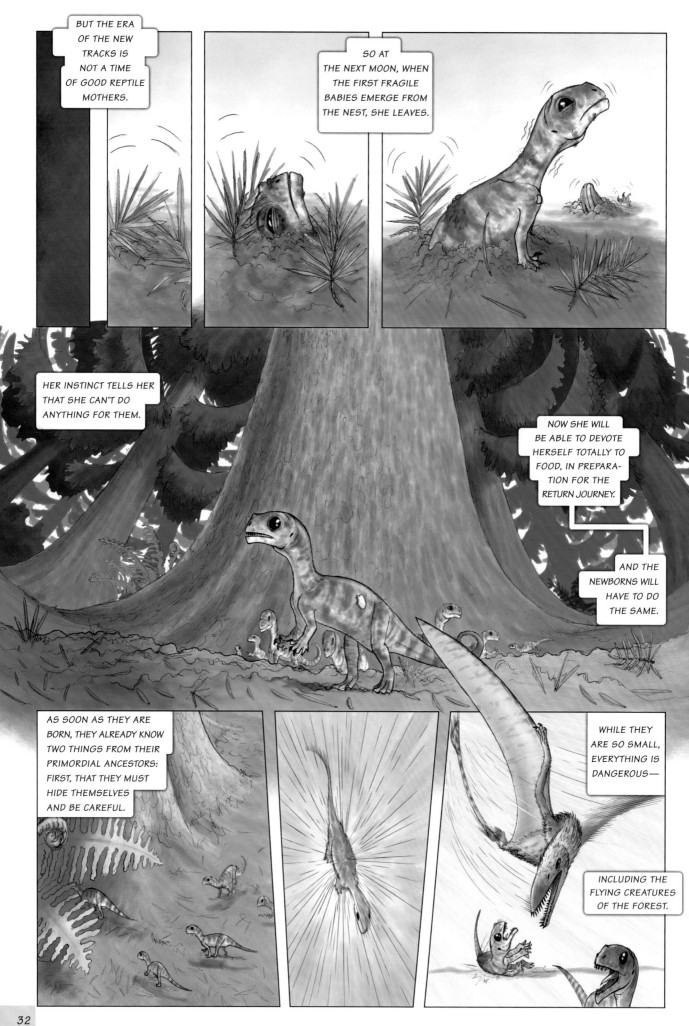

BUT THE ERA OF THE NEW TRACKS IS NOT A TIME OF GOOD REPTILE MOTHERS.

SO AT THE NEXT MOON, WHEN THE FIRST FRAGILE BABIES EMERGE FROM THE NEST, SHE LEAVES.

HER INSTINCT TELLS HER THAT SHE CAN'T DO ANYTHING FOR THEM.

NOW SHE WILL BE ABLE TO DEVOTE HERSELF TOTALLY TO FOOD, IN PREPARATION FOR THE RETURN JOURNEY.

AND THE NEWBORNS WILL HAVE TO DO THE SAME.

AS SOON AS THEY ARE BORN, THEY ALREADY KNOW TWO THINGS FROM THEIR PRIMORDIAL ANCESTORS: FIRST, THAT THEY MUST HIDE THEMSELVES AND BE CAREFUL.

WHILE THEY ARE SO SMALL, EVERYTHING IS DANGEROUS—

INCLUDING THE FLYING CREATURES OF THE FOREST.

THE SECOND THING THEY KNOW IS THAT THEY ARE HUNGRY.

IN THE UNDER-GROWTH, THE LITTLE ONES GREEDILY EAT EVERY SHOOT, BERRY, AND INSECT WITHIN REACH.

ALTHOUGH THEY GROW VERY QUICKLY, THEY HAVE ONLY A FEW MOONS TO BECOME STRONG ENOUGH TO SUCCESSFULLY FACE THE RETURN JOURNEY SOUTH, ALONG WITH THE OTHERS.

THE VALLEYS OF THE NORTH, WITH THEIR RIVERS AND LAKES, GIVE NOURISHMENT TO THE DINOSAURS OVER THE RAINY MONTHS.

BUT THE MOONS PASS, THE WINDS BLOW, AND THE CLOUDS RACE BY,

MAKING THE RAINS INCREASINGLY RARE, EVEN IN THE GREEN GARDENS OF THE NORTHERN REGIONS.

WHEN EVEN THE LEAVES OF THE NORTH TURN YELLOW, THE SIMPLE MINDS ATOP THOSE LONG NECKS INCREASINGLY FEEL AN URGENCY TO DEPART, TO HEAD OUT ONCE AGAIN ON THAT INVISIBLE PATH.

THUS OLD AND YOUNG GENERATIONS ALIKE START MARCHING AGAIN.

GNOOOUU

GNUUU

GNU

GNOU

THE HERD GROWS LARGER AS IT COVERS GROUND, AND ONCE AGAIN THE BEASTS BELLOW TO GREET AND REASSURE EACH OTHER.

SOME WHO WERE THERE BEFORE ARE NO LONGER PRESENT, WHILE MANY FACES ARE NEW, JOINING THE CYCLE OF THE MARCH, AND IT WILL BE UP TO THEM TO MATE DURING THE COMING SEASON.

FIVE YOUNGSTERS REMAIN OF OUR HEROINE'S LITTER.

THE STRUGGLE THROUGH THE UNDERGROWTH IS DIFFICULT...

...EVEN IF THE LITTLE ONES, UNLIKE THE ADULTS, STAY IN A GROUP FOR THE EARLY PART OF THEIR LIVES.

THEY ARE INEXPERIENCED AND ARE ATTRACTED BY TEMPTING BUSHES FAR FROM THE PATH OF THE JOURNEY.

THESE ARE NOT TASTY, BUT FOR THE NAIVE DINOSAURS THE FIRST HUNGER PANGS DURING THE TREK ARE UNBEARABLE.

WHAT THEY DON'T YET KNOW IS THAT BUSHES AND ROCKS CAN HIDE MORTAL DANGERS...

35

RAAHHH!

!!!

WITH A RAUCOUS CRY, THE PREDATORS HURL THEMSELVES UPON THE HUNGRIEST AND MOST CARELESS OF THE SIBLINGS.

HE REARS UP, WAVES HIS CLAWS,

SWOOSH

ZASH

GRR

GRAB!

AND TRIES TO DEFEND HIMSELF,

BUT HIS BLOWS ARE WEAK.

NGWAH!

THE STRUGGLE IS BRIEF.

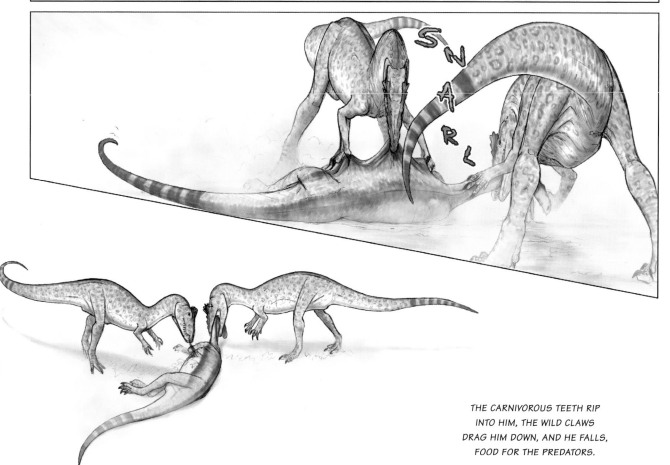

THE CARNIVOROUS TEETH RIP
INTO HIM, THE WILD CLAWS
DRAG HIM DOWN, AND HE FALLS,
FOOD FOR THE PREDATORS.

HIS BROTHERS AND SISTERS,
HAVING MANAGED TO
FLEE, WILL REMEMBER
NOT TO LET THEMSELVES
BE TEMPTED
IN THE FUTURE.

THEY
REJOIN
THE HERD,
MOVING
TOWARD THE
LANDS TO THE
SOUTH...

...TOWARD
FUTURE
ERAS WHEN
THE ANCES-
TRAL MEMORY OF THE
JOURNEY WILL HELP
OTHERS TO
BE STRONGER.

LIFE IS THE MOST BEAUTIFUL INVENTION OF NATURE,

AND DEATH IS ITS WAY OF SUSTAINING YET MORE LIFE.

THE JOURNEY CONTINUES.

DINOSAUR EVOLUTION

This diagram of the evolution of the dinosaurs (in which the red lines represent evolutionary branches for which there is fossil evidence) shows the two principal groups (the saurischians and ornithischians) and their evolutionary path through time during the Mesozoic. Among the saurischians (to the right), we can see the evolution of our heroine's descendants, the sauropodomorphs, who were all herbivores and were the largest animals ever to walk the earth. Farther to the right, still among the saurischians, we find the theropods. Among the theropods there quite soon emerges a line characterized by rigid tails (Tetanurae), from which, through the maniraptors, birds (Aves) evolve. The ornithischians (to the left), which were all herbivores, have an equally complicated evolutionary history, which begins with the basic *Pisanosaurus* type but soon splits into Thyreophora ("shield bearers," such as ankylosaurs and stegosaurs) on the one hand, and Genasauria ("lizards with cheeks") on the other. The latter in turn evolve into two principal lines: the marginocephalians, which include ceratopsians, and euornithopods, which include the most flourishing herbivores of the Mesozoic, the hadrosaurs.

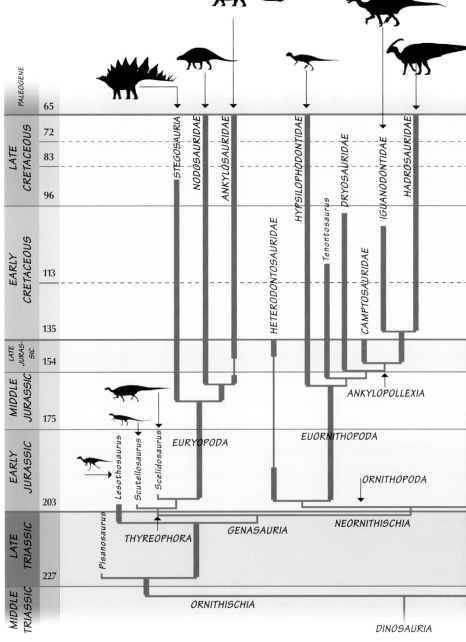

IDENTIKIT *(see page 6)*

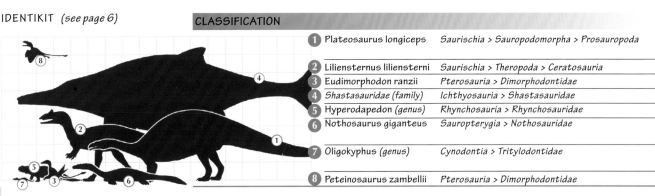

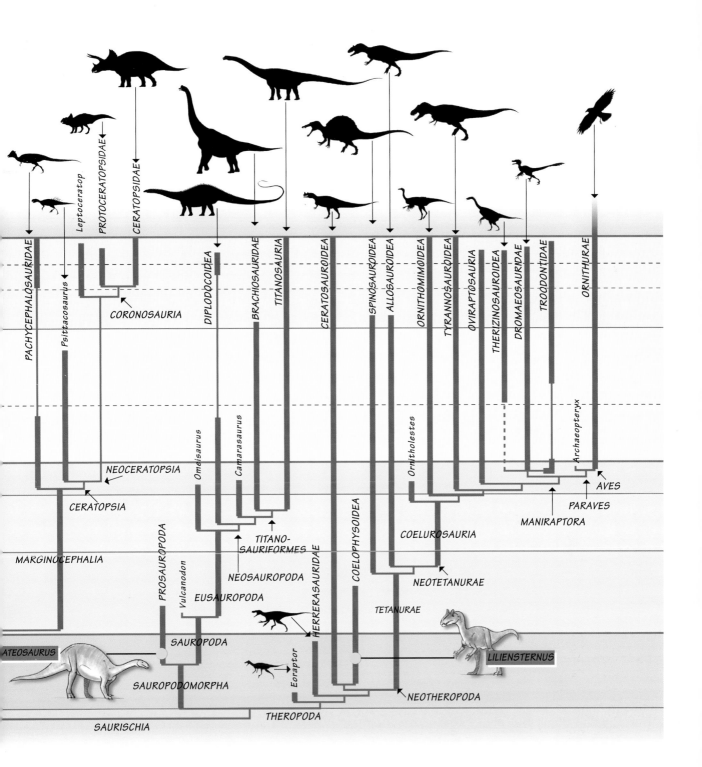

LENGTH	HEIGHT	WEIGHT	DIET	PERIOD	TERRITORY
up to 25 feet	up to 15 feet when upright	up to 2 tons	plants, sometimes insects and small animals	Late Triassic (Middle and Late Norian)	Germany, France, Switzerland, Greenland
over 16 feet	over 5 feet	over 1,100 lbs.	meat	Late Triassic (Late Norian)	Germany
wingspan: over 3 feet		unknown	fish, perhaps insects	Late Triassic (Norian)	Italy
over 30 feet		over 5½ tons	fish and shellfish	Late Triassic (Norian)	from Asia to North America
5 feet		65 to 110 lbs.	plants	Middle and Late Triassic (Norian)	England, India
up to 13 feet		up to 330 to 440 lbs.	fish and shellfish	Middle and Late Triassic (?–Norian)	Germany, France, Switzerland, Russia
over 1½ feet		18 oz.	insects, small animals, eggs	Late Triassic, Early Jurassic	Germany, England, Wales
wingspan: over 3 feet		unknown	insects and small animals	Late Triassic (Norian)	Italy

THE TRIASSIC
NEW TRACKS ON PANGAEA

A Brief History of Life

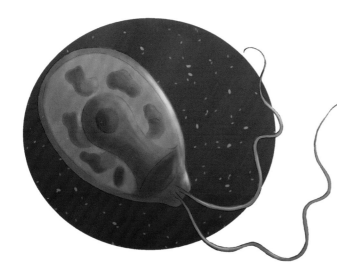

Life is undoubtedly the most important phenomenon in the history of our planet—otherwise we
wouldn't be here to talk about it—and it is a phenomenon that involves many things we don't fully
understand yet, first among these being its origins.
Scholars are still trying to determine how and
why life began on our planet, but in the mean-
time, some of the stages following its appearance
are more clear.

We know that the first certain traces of living
creatures date to over 3 billion years ago, but a
great deal of time elapsed before the appearance
of multicellular organisms that we may consider
animals. And even among these, there are a great
many that present serious problems for paleontologists, the scientists who study past forms
of life. Some have strange shapes with unusual
symmetries, whose outward appearance we know
only through fossils and which may not even
have any living descendants in our time. However,
other organisms continued to evolve, beginning
in these distant times, and we can say that about
500 million years ago, in the Cambrian period,

▲ *We are accustomed
to thinking of unicellular
organisms as primitive,
but the first life-forms
to inhabit Earth, for
hundreds of millions of
years, were even simpler
than this protozoan.*

▶ *The landscape of
Earth shortly after its
formation: erupting
volcanoes, lightning and
rainstorms, and gray and
apparently sterile seas.
The only noises were
those of thunder, waves,
and volcanic eruptions.*

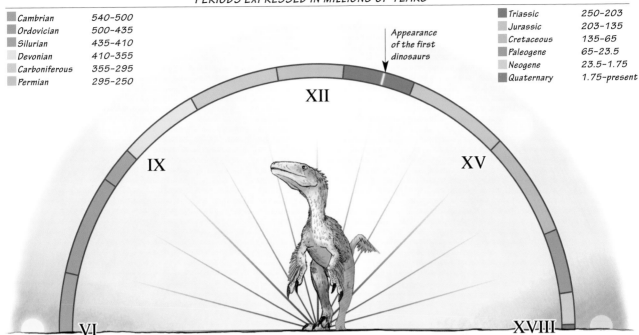

Cambrian	540-500
Ordovician	500-435
Silurian	435-410
Devonian	410-355
Carboniferous	355-295
Permian	295-250

Triassic	250-203
Jurassic	203-135
Cretaceous	135-65
Paleogene	65-23.5
Neogene	23.5-1.75
Quaternary	1.75-present

Appearance of the first dinosaurs

XII

IX

XV

VI

XVIII

▲ If you think of the beginning of the Cambrian period (540 million years ago) as the dawn of a 12-hour day, during which every minute lasts for approximately 750,000 years, the first complex organisms appear shortly after dawn (about 500 million years ago). Life develops throughout the entire morning, and the apocalypse at the end of the Permian period (250 million years ago) takes place at lunchtime, around 12:25. The first dinosaurs appear half an hour later, and their long reign lasts for much of the afternoon, until their extinction at 4:30 p.m. (or 65 million years ago). Mammals inherit Earth as the sun begins to set, and the first men appear only a couple of minutes before dusk, at about 5:58 p.m. From the Cambrian to the Permian period, we are in the Paleozoic era; from the Triassic to the Cretaceous, in the Mesozoic era. The Paleogene, Neogene, and Quaternary, meanwhile, are part of the current Cenozoic era.

there already existed the earliest complex organisms similar to those that live today.

But there were many stages still to be passed through. In fact, the first hundreds of millions of years of the history of life took place in the sea. Meanwhile the land must have been an arid and empty place, where the only noises were those of the wind among the rocks, thunderstorms, and volcanic eruptions (as well as the occasional impact of a meteorite); an additional sound, however, was that of the waves—and it was precisely along the coasts of the primitive seas that the first "steps" were taken toward dry land.

About 410 million years ago, during the Devonian period, the first animals and plants had just begun the adventure of life on land. These were arthropods (the **phylum** that includes invertebrates with exoskeletons, like crabs, shrimp, spiders, and insects) and extremely primitive plants with a very simple structure. The landscape at that time probably was made up mainly of lakes and seas surrounded by a zone of greenish shoreline, and by a few strange-looking low plants, among which the early arthropods moved about, seeking to colonize the lands above sea level. It was precisely during this period that vertebrates probably began to carry out "incursions" from the water onto the land; these were aquatic creatures, some extremely large in size, endowed with very modified fins and numerous fingers (up to eight).

The evolution of life on dry land was quite complex, and we do not know exactly how each step took place, although scholars are quite clear about all the problems that organisms must have had to resolve before moving from water to land. We know, for example, that most of them had to develop new systems for breathing, for walking, for supporting their bodies, for using their senses (which have to be different in the water), for feeding themselves, and for reproducing—the ultimate goal of every organism. And all these problems were brilliantly resolved by both plants and animals, gradually resulting in the variety of forms that we are accustomed to seeing today, almost without taking note of them. It is very easy to forget, for example, how much time was needed for the house cat to develop into the creature that we see today, as it wreaks havoc on our CD collection.

The history of Earth is conventionally divided into eras, which are long periods of time bracketed by two particular events. For example, the Mesozoic era (the era of the dinosaurs) takes place between the largest mass extinction that ever occurred (the Permian crisis) and the second-largest one (the **K-T event** at the end of the Cretaceous period, which we will look at more closely in one of our later books).

These eras are in turn divided into periods. For example, the Mesozoic era is made up of the Triassic, Jurassic, and Cretaceous periods. Each period is then further divided, complicating things even more for paleontologists. And yet it is these divisions that make it easier to put the different pieces of the evolutionary puzzle into place. The task of dividing the past into eras and periods is part of the field known as **stratigraphy**. This geological discipline uses various methods to provide scholars who study the past with an actual timeline that can be used for establishing the order of events. As they say, "It's hard work, but somebody has to do it."

Eras are conventionally grouped into larger units called eons. The story of life on Earth concerns only two eons, and the second one, known as the Phanerozoic, includes the three great eras of life: the Paleozoic, Mesozoic, and Cenozoic. Phanerozoic literally means "visible life," because beginning with the first period of the Phanerozoic, the Cambrian, we have multicellular forms of life visible to the naked eye. In the preceding eon, sometimes called the Cryptozoic, or the time of "hidden life," many of the life-forms known to paleontologists are microscopic organisms.

During the Paleozoic era, the world underwent many changes, and life literally sorted itself out, beginning with simple structures and in certain cases with veritable experiments, and leading up to the principal groups of modern living creatures.

▼ *The millions of years accumulate in layers of rock, like the pages of a book that can be read by expert eyes to reveal fantastic stories and hidden mysteries. These Paleozoic layers were photographed in the southern United States.*

All the **phyla** that exist today appeared by the beginning of the Paleozoic, or probably even before.

By the close of the Paleozoic, the continents were joined together into one great supercontinent called Pangaea and surrounded by a single enormous ocean called Panthalassa. And at the end of the Permian, the final period of the Paleozoic era, Earth was devastated by the greatest catastrophe ever to occur, during which life itself was in danger of disappearing. Thus the Mesozoic era began with a sort of "empty" world, full of opportunity, where the surviving organisms succeeded in colonizing all available spaces, in what scholars call **adaptive radiation**.

In fact, extinction can be seen as a sort of bottleneck, through which only a few organisms among those existing at the moment of extinction can pass. Once they have made it through the bottleneck, these organisms will find many empty places where they will be able to comfortably insert themselves in order to thrive once again. This "bottleneck effect," as scholars call it, is what happened at the end of the Permian, so that the Triassic period began with great opportunities for those few organisms that managed to pass through the terrible tragedy of mass extinction.

▲ *Among the strange organisms that appeared in the Cambrian, the superpredator Anomalocaris was one of the most bizarre. (This is a reconstruction at the Royal Tyrrell Museum in Alberta, Canada.) When only partial specimens were known, its mouth was thought to be a jellyfish; its body, a sponge; and its front appendages, strange shrimp. Only after discovering an entire fossil did paleontologists understand their errors.*

The Continental Triassic

The Triassic, originally called the Trias, may be divided into three epochs: the Early Triassic, Middle Triassic, and Late Triassic. While they all belong to the same period, these three epochs saw notable alterations in the world's flora and fauna, and our story unfolds right at the end of the Late Triassic, precisely when the world witnessed the appearance of the creatures that would dominate the coming periods: the dinosaurs.

While in almost all stratigraphy the Triassic is divided on the basis of events documented in the marine **fossil record**, life on land also underwent considerable changes during this period.

For the first two hundred million years of the history of life on land, ecosystems changed gradually until relationships between predators and prey became stabilized. In practice, this means that during the entire Paleozoic era (the era preceding the appearance of dinosaurs), the world was evolving and all the relationships between animals, plants, and the environment were changing, until they increasingly came to resemble those of the present day.

In the Late Permian, that is, at the end of the Paleozoic era, the appearance of terrestrial vertebrate herbivores completed the picture of the **food web** on Earth. While there would continue to be variations in the structures of plant and herbivore communities throughout the Mesozoic and Cenozoic, at this point the "food chains" stabilized

and became practically identical to those that exist today. The term "food chain," although commonly used, is misleading, because it makes something that is in fact quite complicated seem linear. In reality, the relationships between predators and prey are so complex that in the study of ecology, the usual term is food web; and in fact one should keep in mind that the first predators are the herbivores, which "prey" upon plants.

As we have already mentioned, at the end of the Paleozoic era (at the boundary between the Permian and the Triassic periods), our planet was overwhelmed by the greatest catastrophe it had ever experienced: a profound and terrible biological crisis that brought devastation, sweeping away nearly all existing marine species and well over half of those on land. Life itself almost came to an end, and whatever it was that occurred, if it had gone on a bit longer, we probably would not be here to talk about paleontology. However, if the Permian crisis was a terrible event in the sea, data from dry land indicate something less deadly; clues left in the fossil record of flora reveal that in certain regions of the planet it took something like 25 million years to complete the processes of change in vegetation, and even in geological reckoning 25 million years is quite a long period of time.

In fact, it is possible that some organisms avoided the effects of the Permian crisis and instead only experienced the more long-term effects of the

TRIASSIC	Rhaetian	209–203 mya
	Norian	221–209 mya
	Carnian	227–221 mya
	Ladinian	234–227 mya
	Anisian	242–234 mya
	Scythian	250–242 mya

◀ *The Triassic can be divided into various stages corresponding to stratigraphic levels. This allows for greater precision when paleontologists want to locate in time the fossils they have discovered. Our story unfolds in the Norian, the second-to-last stage of the Triassic. (mya = millions of years ago)*

▶ *A few of today's best-adapted predators of plants. Some herbivores display incredible adaptations, like a compartmentalized stomach and a special way of chewing.*

inevitable **turnover** caused by large-scale climatic and environmental changes.

During the Middle and Late Triassic, Pangaea (the large landmass into which the continents we know today were joined) slowly moved northward. Despite the fact that Pangaea was a single continental mass, paleontologists have noted that terrestrial flora and fauna during the Triassic seem to have been distinctly regional, with differences occurring from zone to zone. The explanation that scientists have found for this phenomenon lies in the seasonal nature of the climate; today we take for granted that there are four seasons, but in the past, the climate was not always so precisely regulated. For example, during the Mesozoic era there probably were only two seasons: the dry season **✱1**, when it did not rain, and the wet season, when it did.

Another cause of regional variations in plants may be found in a climatic situation of the type that is seen in present-day India: the Triassic had a monsoon climate, with strong differences between the seasons, probably because of Pangaea's position, which symmetrically straddled the Equator. Moreover, air masses that stop for long periods over a uniform region, such as a desert or an ocean, assume the characteristics of that zone. This phenomenon is called "characterization of air masses," and it is one of the reasons why it rarely rains in deserts. The fact that Pangaea was a single immense continent likely caused similar phenomena, but on a much broader scale, further influencing the climate of the Triassic.

Pangaea may be divided into two large areas: a northern area, called Laurasia, and a southern area, called Gondwana. These two enormous areas had

▲ The world in the Norian stage of the Triassic. Pangaea is clearly divided into two parts. Our story unfolds in the area circled in red.

characteristic flora and fauna, although, as studies have demonstrated, there are zones in which overlap may be noted (for example, the fossil record of India shows Gondwanan plants living alongside Laurasian animals). However, as one gradually moves forward in the Triassic, these **endemic** types tend to diminish.

The Triassic concluded with another mass extinction, undoubtedly much less striking than that of the Permian. Pangaea was breaking up, and probably this rupture of the supercontinent was one of the causes for the extinction, but there is at least one crater from a meteor impact in Canada that has led some scholars to speculate that the extinction was caused by a large meteorite striking the Earth at the end of the Triassic.

✱1
page 19
panel 5

The Marine Triassic

After the twilight of the Permian period, the situation was certainly no better in the sea than on land. In fact, marine fauna experienced the worst of the Permian mass extinction; scientists calculate that between 90 and 97 percent of existing species vanished.

However, it was precisely during the Triassic "revival" that the dominant marine groups developed.

Among invertebrates, the most important event of the Triassic was the formation of reefs. The first coral reefs were actually hexacorals, since the Paleozoic tetracorals had become extinct at the end of the Permian. Tetracorals and hexacorals are two different groups of, well, corals. The differences between the groups are considerable and have to do with their **morphological** characteristics.

But there were also new animals that began constructing reefs. These were **bivalves**. In fact, at the beginning of the Triassic, the role of reef builder was still unclaimed. The tetracorals were extinct, and the hexacorals were still too "weak" to take on the dominant role that they would later assume, so many groups of invertebrates tried to become reef builders. The most successful of these were undoubtedly certain pteriomorph bivalves (related to present-day pectinoides), which built notable reefs on which an entire community would establish itself, and which would become extinct with the event at the end of the Triassic and the consequent disappearance of the bivalve reefs. These bivalves became prey for some of the most surprising marine reptiles that have ever existed: the placodonts ✱2. Truly bizarre, these creatures had broad and often armor-plated bodies, and resembled turtles, but their skulls were substantially different. Their front teeth were structured to pluck objects from the sea floor (presumably bivalves), and their back teeth, wide and powerful, to crush the shells of their prey.

Placodonts flourished during the Triassic, but probably were closely tied to the bivalve reefs, and in fact also became extinct with the disappearance of the latter.

Ammonites (cephalopod mollusks, distant relatives of present-day squid), on the other hand, benefited from the near-total extinction of the **nautiluses** and spread more extensively; during the Triassic, numerous new forms of ammonites appeared. The ammonites, in turn, probably became prey for other marine animals.

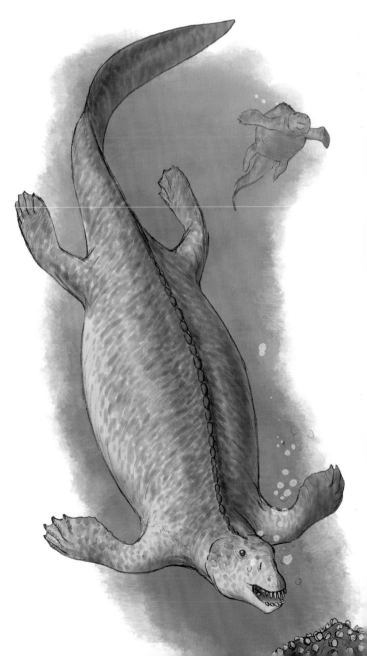

✱2
page 16
panel 6

▶ Placodus was one of the largest placodonts, whose name means "platelike teeth." It lived in the Middle to Late Triassic.

The first ichthyosaurs appeared: these reptiles were thoroughly adapted to marine life and lost their ability to walk on land. The earliest examples, such as *Mixosaurus*, had a tapered body with a long snout, short fins (their four feet), and a long, pointed tail. Toward the end of the Triassic, ichthyosaurs attained formidable dimensions, with animals such as *Shonisaurus* or *Shastasaurus* reaching and perhaps exceeding 50 feet in length. It is interesting to observe that the ichthyosaurs of the Jurassic and Cretaceous, while even more adapted to aquatic life (it was not until the Jurassic that ichthyosaurs would assume their definitive form), would never again attain similar dimensions.

The marine reptiles of the Triassic also included the probable ancestors of the flippered marine reptiles called plesiosaurs: the nothosaurs ✱3.

These were semiaquatic reptiles of average size (they reached up to 13 feet, with an average length of 6 ½ feet, such as the one that appears in our story). Their bodies were elongated and suitable for swimming, thanks to the thrust of their powerful tails; their massive heads, situated at the end of a long, flexible neck, and their teeth were structured for capturing the fish that served as their nourishment. According to some scholars, plesiosaurs, which would thrive beginning in the Late Triassic, had their origins in the nothosaurs.

The pachypleurosaurs were much smaller (from 8 inches to 3 feet long), but otherwise rather similar to the nothosaurs, except for the cranium, which was rounder.

And in the Triassic, amphibians—trematosaurs—also tried to survive in the sea, but with little success. These specialized amphibians bring to mind the modern gharial, a crocodilian from India, in their shape, which featured very elongated snouts and teeth adapted to capturing fish. Their capacity to live in the sea should not be undervalued, since the marine environment was an extremely dangerous place for creatures with their physiology.

Finally, special mention should be made of another animal, about whose lifestyle we are still not very clear: *Tanystropheus*. Probably this was a coastal piscivore, or fish-eater, endowed with an extremely long but not very flexible neck, since it had only a few, very elongated vertebrae. Undoubtedly this is one of the oddest animals of the Triassic.

However, reptiles and amphibians were certainly not the dominant vertebrates in the sea. The true rulers of the waves were fish: such species as the fearful predator *Saurichthys* ✱4 or the squat *Birgeria* ✱5, either with bodies that were still well-armored or with the first "light" forms, precursors of modern fish.

The enormous evolutionary success of sharks, which in the Paleozoic era underwent incredible development, seemed to decline somewhat. In fact, only the hybodonts survived the Permian crisis, experiencing continued evolutionary success during

✱3
page 16
panel 5

✱4
page 15
panel 1

✱5
page 16
panel 1

▶ A cast of a fossil of the skull of Besanosaurus, one of the oldest known ichthyosaurs. Over 20 feet long, it was discovered in Lombardy, Italy, in strata from the Middle Triassic.

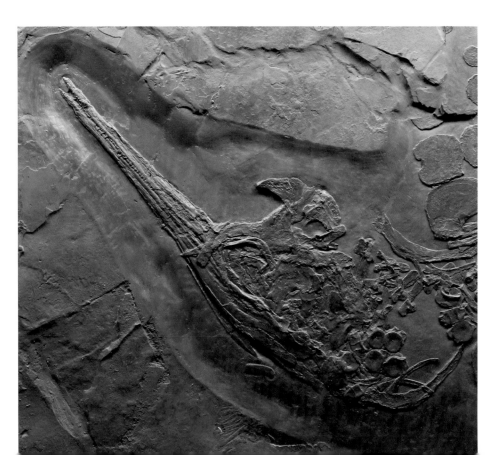

※6
page 15
panel 3

▲ Tanystropheus was quite a bizarre animal, over 13 feet long, whose biology is still not completely understood.

the Triassic, before slowly giving way to the type of shark that would rule the seas, the neoselachians. The hybodonts must have been slow swimmers, but capable of brief rapid spurts, and their teeth were quite varied; some species probably ate fish, others mollusks.

In the Triassic, a second group of aquatic vertebrates—the bony fish—also flourished. Anticipating the triumph of the forms that would characterize the Cenozoic era (and today's seas, since "modern" fish have the most species of all the groups of vertebrates), the first true bony fish, called neopterygians, differentiated into many forms during the Triassic. Some became tapered and rapid swimmers; others maintained their armor and adapted to a slower mode of swimming and to hunting hard and practically motionless prey, such as mollusks or coral. Some of these ancient fish still survive today, such as *Amia*, a large predator that inhabits American rivers.

We can see a large *Ichthyosaurus* in our story ※6, probably a relative of the North American giants. This animal is already perfectly adapted to its environment. Its large, curved tail generates sufficient power to move the animal through the water, and its large eyes are capable of peering into the shadowy depths of the sea, where it hunts down fish and cephalopods, using a snout armed with conical teeth suitable for catching slippery prey. Its four feet are modified into stabilizing fins for moving through the water with agility while hunting.

This majestic sea creature traverses the levels of

salt water in search of its prey, ignoring the small *Nothosaurus*. Because of its bulk, our *Ichthyosaurus* fears very few, if any, creatures, but *Nothosaurus* is not quarry for our enormous aquatic reptile, whose long and narrow jaws are specialized for very different types of food. The sole disadvantage of *Ichthyosaurus* compared to the fish and invertebrates that it eats is that, being a reptile, it is equipped with lungs and therefore must return to the surface in order to breathe. But *Ichthyosaurus* has already definitively abandoned terra firma. It gives birth to its young in the water instead of laying eggs, because at this point its skeleton is incapable of supporting it on land. It is at home in its world of uncertain light and boundless waters.

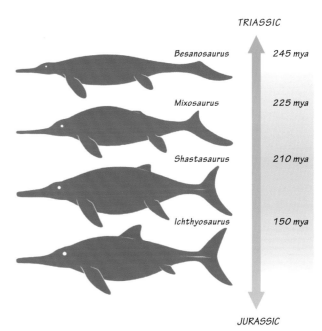

TRIASSIC

Besanosaurus — 245 mya

Mixosaurus — 225 mya

Shastasaurus — 210 mya

Ichthyosaurus — 150 mya

JURASSIC

▲ The ichthyosaurs evolved into forms that were increasingly complex and better adapted to aquatic life. Beginning with a bauplan like that of Besanosaurus, whose body and tail recall those of a reptile, they evolved into forms like the elegant Ichthyosaurus, which was certainly an excellent swimmer, and which, as the Greek root of its name suggests, resembles a fish. (The animals are not drawn to scale.)

Vegetation

The vegetation of the Triassic was different not only from that of the modern world, but also to a certain degree from that of the Paleozoic world. Thus we discover primitive conifers ✳7 (like *Archaeopteris* ✳8) alongside ferns ✳9 (some still treelike) and other plants such as the primitive seed-bearing Cycadales ✳10 and Bennettitales. In northern latitudes, Ginkgoales were abundant (and they are still represented today by *Ginkgo biloba*, which can be seen in many large parks and which produce fruit with a strong smell).

Studies by paleobotanists seem to conclude that there was not yet any **zoochorous** dispersion of plant seeds, because the seeds of the time were structured to be spread by the wind rather than by animals. We also know from fossils that conifers probably represented the majority of tall trees present in the Triassic landscape, along with

Ginkgoales and Cycadales, while the equivalent of our prairies or savannas may have been formed by ferns, and the aquatic zones may have contained large spore-bearing Equisetales ✳11 (some up to 30 feet tall, although present-day Equisetales are very small marsh plants). There is also evidence of coastal vegetation made up of a single plant genus (*Pleuromeia* ✳12, a lycopsid), which lived along estuaries, lakes, and seacoasts. Vegetation was obviously abundant near waterways and in humid regions, but there is much evidence that it also grew at a distance from rivers and lakes.

✳9
page 23
panel 2

✳10
page 21
center

✳7
page 34
panel 2

✳8
page 20
panel 4

✳11
page 30
panel 4

✳12
page 20
panel 2

Terrestrial Fauna

In the Triassic, terrestrial animal life was quite varied.

Among invertebrates, there were at least four orders of insects that still survived from the Paleozoic era (including beetles, and the ancestors of grasshoppers and cicadas), and the first examples of Phasmida (stick insects) made their appearance. It should be noted that while invertebrates thrived in aquatic environments, they colonized the land only in very small groups, and even these—with the exception of arthropods—would remain tied to the water. Terrestrial invertebrates that are not arthropods include gastropods (snails and slugs) and anellids (earthworms).

As for vertebrates during the Triassic, synapsids (so-called "mammalian reptiles") declined compared to diapsids (the group of reptiles that includes dinosaurs, lizards, and the flying reptiles called pterosaurs). One of the causes for this might be

sought in their different types of **excretion**. According to some scholars, in fact, the evidence for an increase in **xerophilous** plants might indicate a drying up of the climate, with the result that synapsids, which probably were ureotelic (that is, they excreted nitrogen wastes as urea, which means they lost more water), would have been less efficient than diapsids, which, instead, were uricotelic (that is, they excreted uric acid and thus lost less water).

Some fauna were curiously limited in size. For example, the well-known *Lystrosaurus*, in South Africa, was smaller than in the Permian period, attaining a maximum length of 6½ feet.

However, these limitations vanished with the appearance of the first herbivorous dinosaurs.

The most typical and widespread herbivores included dicynodonts, the best-known example of which is *Lystrosaurus*. These were squat quadrupeds, endowed with a large cranium,

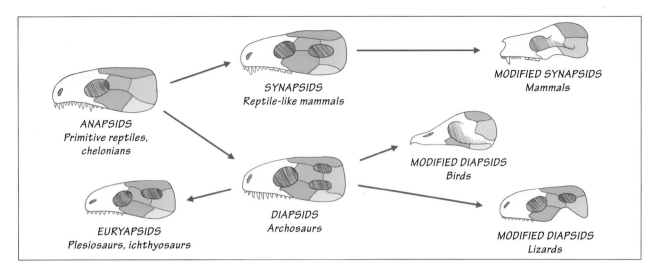

ANAPSIDS
Primitive reptiles,
chelonians

SYNAPSIDS
Reptile-like mammals

MODIFIED SYNAPSIDS
Mammals

MODIFIED DIAPSIDS
Birds

DIAPSIDS
Archosaurs

EURYAPSIDS
Plesiosaurs, ichthyosaurs

MODIFIED DIAPSIDS
Lizards

▲ The reptilian cranium has undergone considerable modifications from the Carboniferous period to the present. The first reptiles had a compact skull without any post-orbital openings, or openings behind the eye socket, and thus they are called anapsids. Present-day turtle and tortoise skulls still look this way. The line that led to mammals, that of the synapsids, is characterized by a single post-orbital opening and by a substantial reduction in the number of cranial bones, as well as by a change in the jaw joint: in mammals, the two principal bones of the reptilian jaw, the quadrate and the articular, become part of the structure of the ear. The central line shown here is undoubtedly the one that flourished most successfully. Diapsids, which take their name from the presence of two post-orbital openings, evolved into dinosaurs and birds on the one hand, and "modern" reptiles on the other. One particular form of diapsid is that of the marine reptiles called euryapsids. They appear to have only one post-orbital opening, but in reality the second one has been closed up by considerable changes in the lower portion of the cranium.

almost completely toothless but equipped with a strong, horny beak for cutting plants, and they were wide-ranging in Gondwana (the southern portion of the supercontinent Pangaea). Other large herbivores included various types of cynodonts (synapsids that were **heterodont**, or equipped with teeth of different shapes), which could grow as long as 10 feet and were able to eat rather hard vegetation.

However, it is the archosaurs (which were diapsids) that stand out among the herbivores. The first

✱13
page 19
panel 4

group of archosaurs that we encounter is that of the rhynchocephalians (to which the *Hyperodapedon* ✱13 in our story also belongs), which were also quite widespread on Gondwana. These were some of the most flourishing forms in the Triassic, thanks to their system of mastication, or chewing. The entire cranium was structured for a sort of cutting mastication that allowed the rhynchocephalians to attack different types of plants, and the structure of their feet also suggests that these herbivores were able to dig and unearth roots.

Herbivorous archosaurs also included stagonolepids (a sort of armored herbivorous crocodile), procolophonids (small quadrupeds with a powerful bite), and trilophosaurs (equipped with a horny beak).

However, the most distinctive thing about the Triassic was undoubtedly the appearance of the first dinosaurs. The herbivores included prosauropods, such as the *Plateosaurus* in our story, and the first small ornithischians.

From an ecological standpoint, we can recognize two distinct phases for the herbivores of the Triassic. The first ones had relatively small bodies, with skulls structured for powerful bites and

◄ Lystrosaurus was a large herbivorous marsh reptile, typical of Gondwana; it was over 3 feet long. In the Karoo region of South Africa, its fossils are so common that it is possible to run across several complete Lystrosaurus skulls on a single day's walk.

adequate mastication; they could feed only up to limited heights (about 3 feet from the ground). The second group of herbivores, the prosauropods, were larger in mass and body size and could nibble at greater heights. They were characterized not by skulls specialized to process vegetation (that is, to carry out all the necessary operations, from gathering to digesting plants), but rather by skulls structured only to gather food, which was processed by the stomach instead.

Among the carnivores, such archosaurs as the crocodiles soon became the dominant species, at least until the arrival of the **theropod** dinosaurs. Some forms of primitive crocodiles were very well adapted to different environments, and in the Triassic there were also terrestrial crocodiles, large predators that must have terrorized the Triassic herbivores. Some, such as *Postosuchus* (a beast about 15 feet long), had a cranium that greatly resembled that of the more famous *Tyrannosaurus*, and must have been a truly fearful predator. And it was from forms similar to crocodiles that dinosaurs evolved.

But synapsids, at least at the beginning of the Triassic, did not simply stand on the sidelines watching, and they developed predatory forms that were equally frightening, only much smaller (although some were large enough to represent a danger to the big herbivores). These included the therocephalians—some of which were herbivores—and above all the cynodonts (such as *Oligokyphus* ✳**14**), animals that were small but "on a mission." In fact, these were the ancestors of the mammals, which would one day dominate terra firma.

Finally, the air was still almost unknown territory for vertebrates, but during the Triassic the first examples of one of the most fascinating groups of fossil vertebrates evolved: pterosaurs.

These "dragons of the air," as the great paleontologist Harry G. Seeley called them, were among the most astonishing forms ever to have evolved. We will visit them in greater detail in our next book, but for now it suffices to know that these animals had large membranous wings supported by the specialized fourth finger of their hands, which was very long. The body was rather small, often much smaller than the head, while the cranium was specialized for gathering food and for sensory input. In certain cases, it has been possible to study the shape of the brain of these animals, and we have learned that pterosaurs were endowed with considerable visual capacity.

The first pterosaurs, like those in our story, appeared in the Late Triassic in northern Italy and were small, probably piscivorous animals. We do not know what creatures they evolved from, but we do know that from the time pterosaurs appeared in the fossil record, they already had all the typical

✳**14**
page 31
panel 7

▼ *Like all the large "terrestrial crocodiles," Postosuchus was a deadly predator. Its cranium was adapted to withstand considerable stress from impacts with its prey.*

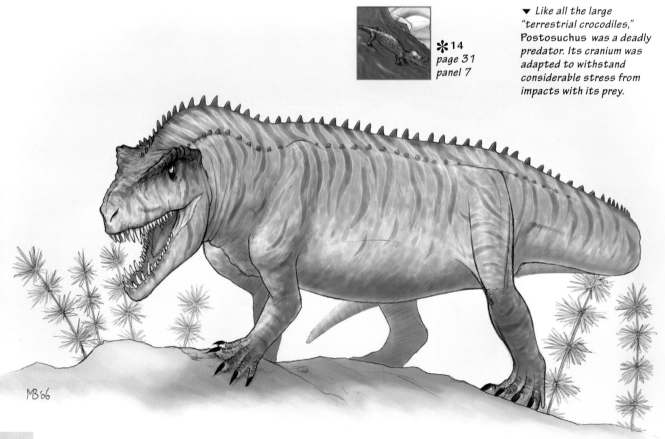

MB'66

characteristics of flying animals, characteristics they would retain throughout their long and glorious history.

Eudimorphodon ✳15, the pterosaur that we see in our story, was a small animal, likely piscivorous. It had teeth of two different types in its jaws (hence its name, which means "teeth of two shapes"). Its wings could transport the animal in the air both by flapping and by gliding. It is possible that pterosaurs utilized both systems, gliding for most of the time in order to conserve energy. In fact, flight is an extremely wasteful activity from the point of view of energy, and it is thus plausible to think that pterosaurs conserved energy whenever possible, exactly as modern marine birds or modern raptors do.

The interpretation of the behavior of an extinct animal based on the way similar living animals act is an approach often employed in paleoecology, and is founded in part on a fundamental principle of the earth sciences, the **principle of actualism.**

Along with *Eudimorphodon*, two other pterosaurs that lived in northern Italy during the Triassic period have been discovered. One is *Peteinosaurus* ✳16 and the other is *Preondactylus*. Both are smaller than *Eudimorphodon* and were probably also fish-eaters. We can imagine the coastal areas of this era, patrolled by these new animals that

had colonized even the last element that had remained free of vertebrates: the air.

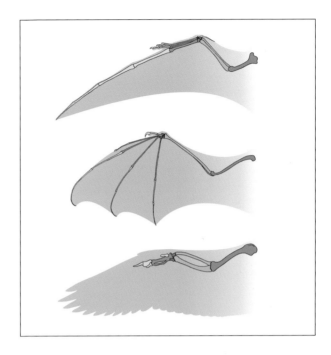

▲ *From top to bottom, the wings of a pterosaur, a bat, and a bird. The first two animals have "opted" for a similar solution, a wing membrane of skin supported by the fingers (in pterosaurs only by the fourth finger, in bats by four fingers), while birds employ the more versatile feathered wing, with an extreme reduction of the fingers but a great increase in flexibility of use and robustness—in fact, birds' wings cannot be torn.*

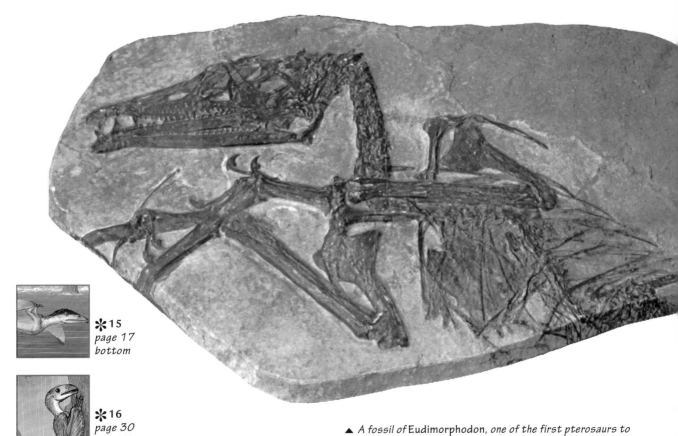

✳15
page 17
bottom

✳16
page 30
panel 7

▲ *A fossil of* Eudimorphodon, *one of the first pterosaurs to evolve, with a wingspan of about 3 feet.*

Dinosaurs

Toward the end of the Triassic, a new biological crisis arose, yet again disturbing this era of upheavals. During this crisis, many groups of terrestrial animals became extinct, and the mammalian reptiles (synapsids) and archosaurs (such as the rhynchocephalians) had to give way to a new race, endowed with the latest "technological advances": dinosaurs.

Two theories are usually proposed for the flourishing of dinosaurs during the Triassic. According to the first theory, dinosaurs were superior in "design" to other reptiles of the time, and therefore their predominance was an almost obvious outcome. With their superior equipment, dinosaurs would have driven off the other reptiles. Alternatively, the second theory states that while dinosaurs were optimally equipped, their success was due only to their ability to benefit from the extinction that was taking place around them. From a practical standpoint, dinosaurs found themselves in the right place at the right time, somewhat as we mammals did when the dinosaurs themselves became extinct at the end of the Cretaceous period.

At the moment, the second theory seems to be more in favor, but we must remember that paleontology is a dynamic science, and even a single new discovery could rewrite history as we know it.

In any case, from the Late Triassic onward, dinosaurs would be the true protagonists of the grand theater of life on land. But what were the structural innovations that these animals built their success on?

Dinosaurs had various features in their **Bauplan**, or body plan, that other reptiles did not have. This made them not only competitive, but indeed victorious within the setting of the Mesozoic era—and, as far as we know, in comparison not only to reptiles, but also to the first mammals.

The first characteristic that made dinosaurs "new" from a structural standpoint, and which is visible even from their skeletons, was the position of their feet.

Reptiles usually hold their feet perpendicular to their bodies, in what is called a *sprawling* posture. In this position, the limbs cannot maintain a rapid

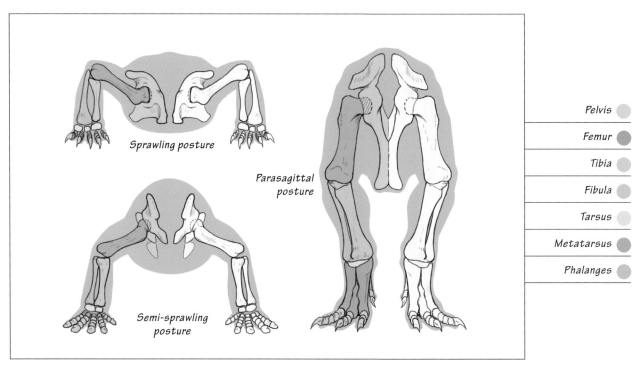

Sprawling posture

Semi-sprawling posture

Parasagittal posture

Pelvis
Femur
Tibia
Fibula
Tarsus
Metatarsus
Phalanges

▲ Reptiles have developed various postures, that is, positions of the feet in relation to the body. The most primitive, which can still be seen today in lizards, is called the sprawling posture and is characterized by the feet being held at a right angle to the body. This means that the entire pelvic or pectoral girdle must move with every step, which is not a very efficient system for moving on dry land. In certain synapsid reptiles, the posture has already become semi-sprawling: the feet are held at an angle to the body, for a more rapid gait that wastes less energy. The best posture, however, is that of dinosaurs and mammals, which wastes the least energy and is the most efficient in terms of movement: the parasagittal posture, in which the feet are held straight beneath the body.

and sustained gait (although they can achieve brief spurts of speed, as in lizards); some more evolved reptiles, such as crocodiles, can move for brief stretches in a gait that is called *semi-sprawling*, where the limbs are held at an oblique angle to the body. This gait, however, can only be maintained for brief periods.

In contrast, dinosaurs had feet set below their bodies, like humans. This type of posture is called *parasagittal*, and allows a wide variety of maneuvers that the other two postures do not. This was undoubtedly the first advantage of the dinosaurs. Moreover, this posture leads to a second advantage: the erect position. The earliest dinosaurs were bipeds; they walked on two feet like their close relatives, such as *Lagosuchus* or *Marasuchus*. They were much quicker and more "multifunctional" than other reptiles of the time.

The metabolism of dinosaurs has also been the subject of frequent debate. Today it is generally thought that dinosaurs had a metabolism very different from that of reptiles and more like that of birds (after all, birds are dinosaurs) or mammals. (We will discuss this topic at length in future volumes.) This would also clearly represent an advantage in a world of "cold-blooded" animals.

Yet despite these advantages, dinosaurs, as we

have already mentioned, probably did nothing other than benefit from a moment when, once again, the world had experienced a great extinction. In short, in addition to being the best, they were also excellent opportunists—like certain soccer forwards!

Only one thing remains to be clarified: what makes a dinosaur a dinosaur? That is, how can we say that a particular animal is a dinosaur or not? Paleontologists use a list of technical features to distinguish dinosaurs from other reptiles. The most important of these features are a peculiar configuration of the joint that connects the femur to the pelvis, which is called the *acetabulum*, and which in dinosaurs is perforated, thereby allowing tremendous mobility of the rear foot; and a very specific configuration of the "ankle," which is better adapted to movement.

It should be said that apart from these common features, dinosaurs would appear in an incredible variety of shapes, truly earning the title that scientists and laymen alike have given them: Lords of Creation.

One constant that allows scholars to classify dinosaurs is the shape of their pelvis. According to the general configuration of the three bones that make up the pelvis (the ilium, ischium, and pubis),

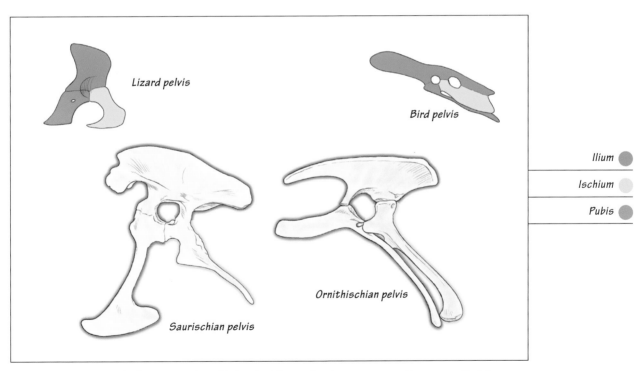

Lizard pelvis

Bird pelvis

Ilium

Ischium

Pubis

Saurischian pelvis

Ornithischian pelvis

▲ Dinosaurs are classified into two large groups, based on the structure of their pelvis. The pelvic bones are called the ilium, the ischium, and the pubis. To the left is a saurischian pelvis, with a three-pronged structure in which the pubis is tilted forward and the ischium backward. This arrangement of the bones is also found in reptiles (upper left). To the right is an ornithischian pelvis, where the ischium and pubis both point backward, and there is a pre-pubic process, that is, a projection in front of the pubis. A similar configuration began to appear in advanced theropods, which then evolved into actual birds (upper right).

we can divide dinosaurs into saurischians and ornithischians. The former have a pelvis with a reptilian structure, where the pubis juts forward while the ischium projects backward (the ilium is parallel to the ground). In ornithischians, however, the ischium and pubis both point backward and are parallel.

Although there are exceptions to this rule (which we shall see in later volumes), these two major subdivisions generally remain clear and distinct throughout the evolutionary history of the dinosaurs. Moreover, as far as we know, all ornithischians were herbivores, and thus carnivores were exclusively saurischians (although among the saurischians there were also herbivores, including the gigantic sauropods, which we'll meet in future volumes).

Where did the dinosaurs come from? As we have seen, the Triassic witnessed a great increase in crocodiles. Among these, paleontologists have assigned some particular forms to a family called Lagosuchidae, including the two bipedal types mentioned earlier, *Lagosuchus* and *Marasuchus*. These are characterized by a delicate, light body, probably adapted to rapid or abrupt movements. The rear feet are larger than the front ones (thus the name of the group, which signifies "rabbit-crocodile"), and it is thought that dinosaurs are descended from these animals.

At the moment that our story unfolds, dinosaurs have started to become established, and they exist in various forms. In fact, the earliest true dinosaurs we know about, such as the Argentinian *Herrerasaurus* and *Eoraptor*, are already more or less past memories, and the evolution and spread of these spectacular creatures throughout the planet is in full swing. The large groups into which paleontologists subdivide dinosaurs may already be distinguished, as we have seen, based on the shape of the pelvis.

Among saurischians, both sauropodomorphs (long-necked herbivorous dinosaurs) and theropods (bipedal carnivorous dinosaurs) are evolving. The former include prosauropods, which encompass types such as *Massospondylus* or *Plateosaurus*—the latter being the protagonist of our story. Meanwhile, at this point theropods have relatively small, slender shapes and are almost certainly agile predators. One of the most well-known early theropods is *Coelophysis bauri*. This North American carnivore became famous when it was first discovered at Ghost Ranch in Texas. Various complete skeletons were found here, and among the rib bones of some were smaller bones, possibly of prey. Until 2006, it was thought that these prey were the babies of *Coelophysis*, but ongoing research has

▶ Marasuchus.
Along with Lagosuchus, *this small archosaur (some 8 inches long), from the Late Triassic in Argentina, is a precursor to the dinosaurs. It is characterized by bipedalism, which we will find in all theropods, and which seems to be a primitive feature of the dinosaurs.*

disproved this terrible image of the cannibal-dinosaur.

Unlike saurischians, ornithischians are not yet so widespread in the Triassic. Probably the most famous Triassic ornithischian is *Fabrosaurus*, discovered in South Africa. Its renown is paradoxical, because unfortunately this animal is known only from a mandible fragment with some teeth, and many paleontologists think that in reality, *Fabrosaurus* may be identified as *Lesothosaurus*, another small ornithischian that lived in the same regions, but which is not otherwise known until the Early Jurassic. If we use our knowledge of *Lesothosaurus* to hypothesize about the characteristics of *Fabrosaurus*, then we may say that the latter was a small herbivore about 3 feet long, bipedal, and equipped with a horny beak that it used to gather the plants it ate. The structure of the rear feet leads us to believe that *Fabrosaurus* was a swift runner. We still know very little about the Triassic ornithischians, although there have been discoveries of animals that are more complete than *Fabrosaurus*, such as *Pisanosaurus*, found in Argentina. The latter seems to have been very primitive, but probably was already equipped with cheek pockets like those found later in the ornithischians of the Jurassic and Cretaceous periods.

But let's take a closer look at the dinosaurs from

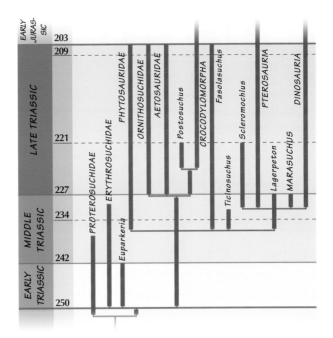

▲ *Dinosaurs are part of the larger group of archosaurs ("ruling reptiles"). Although almost all archosaurs must have resembled crocodiles externally, and almost all were carnivores, two groups of archosaurs were extremely different: pterosaurs, which were the first vertebrates to acquire active flight; and dinosaurs. However, the phylogeny, that is, the precise relationships among the various groups of archosaurs, is still not entirely clear.*

▼ *Discovered in Argentina, the Late Triassic* Herrerasaurus *is the first large carnivorous dinosaur, a predator about 10 feet long, armed with powerful teeth.*

our story. The principal protagonist of the long journey is *Plateosaurus* ✱**17**. From a technical standpoint, this dinosaur is considered primitive; it belongs to the prosauropod group and is related to the large sauropods—the gigantic quadrupedal dinosaurs with long necks, such as *Apatosaurus*, which will appear in the Jurassic. According to some recent studies, prosauropods might also be related to theropods and might be thought of, in evolutionary terms, as "all-purpose" ancestors that could have evolved in more than one direction. Further studies will be needed to clarify their relationship with dinosaurs that come later.

Plateosaurus was a large animal, a true giant for its time, over 20 feet long. Its cranium was not very large, but it was quite robust and had jaws with teeth suitable for cutting the plants that it ate.

Like many of its relatives, *Plateosaurus* could move about easily on all four feet, but when necessary it could use just its two rear feet. Technically speaking, the ability of a normally quadrupedal animal to walk as a biped if necessary is called *faculative bipedism*. To give a present-day example, gorillas and bears are faculative bipeds, but *Plateosaurus* must have been more skilled at walking on two feet than these two animals.

Another characteristic of *Plateosaurus*, which we discover in all prosauropods, is its claws. In fact, this animal had large curved claws, the shape of which quite closely resembles those of predators. Yet our prosauropod was not a carnivore. Some paleontologists suspect that prosauropods were omnivores rather than herbivores, but this still does not completely explain the presence of its formidable claws. Perhaps it used them to defend itself, or perhaps to scrape the bark of trees in search of insect larvae that could supplement its diet.

How did *Plateosaurus* eat? Given the shape of its teeth, and the fact that its cranium does not offer

▲ The little Fabrosaurus is one of the first ornithischian dinosaurs; it will lose its bipedalism during its evolution. Fabrosaurus is herbivorous, although its teeth do not yet have the levels of specialization that will allow ornithischian animals to evolve so successfully. This reconstruction is based on the similar Lesothosaurus.

✱17
page 20
center

◀ A fossil of Coelophysis, a theropod dinosaur about 10 feet long.

▲ A fossil of Plateosaurus, the protagonist of our story. The detail of the skull shows its nonspecialized teeth, presumably capable of "harvesting" plant material.

✻18
page 31
panel 3

evidence of strong muscles, we can suppose with a good degree of certainty that this large herbivore tore up the plants it ate and swallowed them with very little or no mouth activity. (We know that it did not chew, or did so very little and badly.) It is possible that the muscular activity and the gastric juices in its stomach then reduced the food to substances that could be assimilated, just as with today's herbivores, and Jurassic sauropods as well. Perhaps animals such as *Plateosaurus* also swallowed stones (which in this case are called *gastroliths*) to aid in their digestion, precisely as some modern birds do and, as we know, sauropods also did.

Like all dinosaurs known to us, *Plateosaurus* was oviparous, that is, it laid eggs ✻18 from which its young were born. *Plateosaurus* babies could follow their parents or catch their food on their own. We know practically nothing about parental care in these early dinosaurs, and we can only speculate

whether they defended and raised their young or left them to their fate, as in our story.

Whereas we know a great deal about the anatomy of *Plateosaurus*, thanks to the discovery of many examples of this animal, we do not know much about the large theropod we see in our story. This is *Liliensternus* ✻19, an animal about 16 feet long. (The examples in our story are not yet adults and are therefore only about 13 feet long.)

Liliensternus is a primitive carnivorous dinosaur related to the most famous Jurassic predator, *Dilophosaurus*. Unfortunately, the skeletal remains of this Triassic carnivore are fragmentary, particularly the cranium. Moreover, we know relatively little even about its less fragmentary relative *Dilophosaurus*, including, for example, the function of the two famous crests on its snout.

Some paleontologists maintain that *Liliensternus* must also have had at least one crest on its cranium.

We know that it was an *obligate biped* (the opposite of a facultative biped), for it could only walk on its rear feet and could not use its front limbs for locomotion, and from its laterally compressed and curved teeth we know that it must have had a meat-based diet.

Unfortunately we know nothing more, and here too we must base our assumptions on the principle of actualism, as we have done for the pterosaurs, in order to try to understand what type of existence this animal had. Certainly it must have hunted, and its prey clearly included animals of various sizes. It is highly probable that it also hunted young or sick *Plateosaurus*, and it is possible that it hunted in groups—or at least with a partner ✱20.

We have very little evidence concerning theropod babies, and almost none concerning those of primitive theropods. We don't know if the behav-ior of the hatchlings in our story was also exhibited by young *Liliensternus*, but we do know that this carnivore also laid eggs, and we think that its young were able to procure food on their own—yet this too is a mystery that will only be resolved by exceptional discoveries.

Triassic dinosaurs inhabited a completely new world. Animals were, in a certain way, "experimenting" with new solutions on a new planet that had only recently recovered from a terrible catastrophe and was going through a period of only slightly less dreadful ones. At this juncture, dinosaurs knew best how to leverage their abilities, to put it in human terms, and they finally began what would be a very long-lived dynasty, undoubtedly the longest-lived in the history of vertebrates on Earth—one that would culminate in the evolution of birds, as we shall see in our next story ✱21.

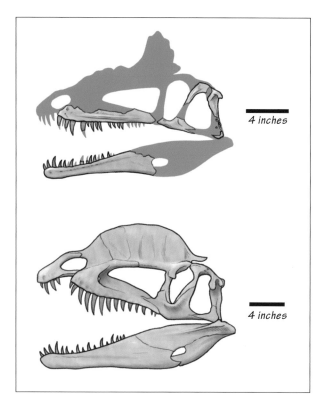

▲ *Above, a reconstruction of the skull of* Liliensternus *(with the missing parts in blue), based on the skulls of two Early Jurassic theropods:* Dilophosaurus, *whose skull is shown below; and the little-known* Cryolophosaurus, *whose fossil remains were discovered in Antarctica.*

✱19
page 36
panel 2

✱20
page 37
panel 2

✱21
Volume 2
A Jurassic Mystery: Archaeopteryx

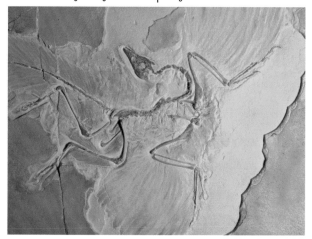

GLOSSARY

Adaptive radiation: the division of one evolutionary line into many lines, to occupy different ecological "spaces."

Bauplan: German for "construction plan"; the structural plan, or basic scheme, of the shape of an organism.

Bivalve: any one of a class of mollusks, exclusively aquatic and mostly saltwater, characterized by the presence of two valves, or shells, and by a muscular foot.

Endemic: living only in a defined place and typical of it; for example, the kangaroo is endemic to Australia.

Excretion: the expulsion of noxious substances (mostly composed of nitrogen) from the body.

Food web: the network of relationships among the organisms of an ecosystem, with the producers (plants) at the base and the superpredators (those predators that are not preyed upon by any other creatures) at the top.

Fossil record: the information about life in the past that is preserved in geological deposits.

Heterodont: "with diverse teeth"; having teeth of different shapes; for example, humans are heterodonts.

K-T event: from the German initials for *Cretaceous* and *Tertiary*; the name for the mass extinction 65 million years ago.

Morphological: concerning the configuration and shape of an organism.

Nautilus: any one of a group of cephalopod mollusks characterized by a shell divided into chambers with a central siphon and a body equipped with a head and tentacles.

Phylum (*pl.* Phyla): the group of all the organisms endowed with a common *bauplan* (structural plan); the taxonomic classification lower than kingdom and higher than class.

Principle of actualism: the idea that if a geological or biological process occurs in a certain way today, it occurred in the same way in the past as well; also called *uniformitarianism*.

Stratigraphy: the branch of the earth sciences that identifies the order and relationships of eras and periods through the study of strata, or layered geological deposits.

Theropod: any one of a group of saurischian dinosaurs, all bipeds and almost all carnivores.

Turnover: change in fauna, flora, or a population.

Xerophilous: growing in or adapted to living in an arid climate.

Zoochory: the dispersion of plant seeds by animals; for example, by seeds becoming attached to the fur.

Acknowledgments

For their help and support both direct and indirect, Matteo Bacchin would like to thank (in no particular order) Marco Signore; Luis V. Rey; Eric Buffetaut; Silvio Renesto; Sante Bagnoli; Joshua Volpara; his dear friends Mac, Stefano, Michea, Pierre, and Santino; and everybody at Jurassic Park Italia. But he thanks above all his mother, his father, and Greta, for the unconditional love, support, and feedback that have allowed him to realize this dream.

Marco Signore would like to thank his parents, his family, Marilena, Enrico di Torino, Sara, his Chosen Ones (Claudio, Rino, and Vincenzo), la Compagnia della Rosa e della Spada, Luis V. Rey, and everybody who has believed in him.

DINOSAURS

1 THE JOURNEY: *Plateosaurus*

We follow the path of a great herd of *Plateosaurus* from the sea—populated by ichthyosaurs—through the desert and mountains, to their nesting places. Their trek takes place beneath skies plied by the pterosaur *Eudimorphodon*, and under the watchful eye of the predator *Liliensternus*.

We discover what life was like on our planet during the Triassic period, and how the dinosaurs evolved.

(In bookstores now)

2 A JURASSIC MYSTERY: *Archaeopteryx*

What killed the colorfully plumed *Archaeopteryx*? Against the backdrop of a great tropical storm, we search for the perpetrator among the animals that populate a Jurassic lagoon, such as the small carnivore *Juravenator*, the pterosaur *Pterodactylus*, crocodiles, and prehistoric fish.

We discover how dinosaurs spread throughout the world in the Jurassic period and learned to fly, and how a paleontologist interprets fossils.

(In bookstores now)

3 THE HUNTING PACK: *Allosaurus*

We see how life unfolds in a herd of *Allosaurus* led by an enormous and ancient male, as they hunt *Camarasaurus* and the armored *Stegosaurus* in groups, look after their young, and struggle amongst themselves. A young and powerful *Allosaurus* forces its way into the old leader's harem. How will the confrontation end?

We discover one of the most spectacular ecosystems in the history of the Earth: the Morrison Formation in North America.

(Coming in Spring 2009)